# Tales of Toyland & Other Stories

## By Enid Blyton

Tales of Toyland & Other Stories
By Enid Blyton

First published in Great Britain by George Newnes in 1944
This edition published 2003 by
Hinkler Books Pty Ltd
17–23 Redwood Drive
Dingley VIC 3172
Australia
www.hinklerbooks.com

www.blyton.com

ISBN 1 8651 5858 5

Printed & bound in Australia

# The Author
## *Enid Blyton*

Enid Blyton is one of the best-loved writers of the twentieth century. Her wonderful, inventive stories, plays and poems have delighted children of all ages for generations.

Born in London in 1897, Enid Blyton sold her first piece of literature; a poem entitled 'Have You ...?', at the age of twenty. She qualified and worked as a teacher, writing extensively in her spare time. She sold short stories and poems to various magazines and her first book, *Child Whispers*, was published in 1922.

Over the next 40 years, Blyton would publish on average fifteen books a year. Some of her more famous works include Noddy, The Famous Five, The Secret Seven and The Faraway Tree series.

Her books have sold in the millions and have been translated into many languages. Enid Blyton married twice and had two daughters. She died in 1968, but her work continues to live on.

# Contents

*Jumping on the hat*

# The Poor Fairy Doll

Once upon a time there was a sailor doll who lived with many other toys in a big nursery. He had a very smiling face and he wore a smart blue velvet suit, and a sailor's cap.

He was always singing. He sang this song:

> *'Yoho for a life on the sea,*
> *Yoho, that's the life for me!*
> *I wish I'd a ship*
> *For I'd take a long trip,*
> *Yoho for a life on the sea!*
> *YOHO!'*

He always sang the last 'yoho' very loudly indeed and the other toys often felt cross with him.

'Sailor, stop yohoing, do!' begged the teddy bear. 'I'm tired of that song.'

'I wish you *would* get a ship and go for a trip,' grumbled the rag doll.

'I'm tired of you, smiling and singing all day long as if you were as happy as a blackbird in spring.'

'Well, I am,' said the sailor doll in surprise. 'Aren't you?'

'Of course not,' said the rag doll gloomily. 'My dress is torn and that makes me feel miserable.'

'And I've got a little hole in my front just here,' said the teddy. 'I leak sawdust out of it and it worries me. I don't feel a bit like singing and laughing. So do be quiet.'

The golden-haired doll and the blue rabbit nodded their heads. They wanted Sailor to be quiet too. The golden-haired doll had lost one of her blue shoes and she was unhappy about it. The blue rabbit had a loose tail and he was afraid it was going to drop off. So nobody except the sailor doll felt very cheerful.

Sailor stopped singing. He almost stopped smiling, but he couldn't quite manage to do that because his face was made that way, with a wide smile. But he did wish that he could have a friend among the toys, who would share a joke with him and be jolly and friendly.

Then, at Christmas time, a new doll came to the nursery toy cupboard. It was the fairy doll off the top of the Christmas tree! She had been given to Sally, the little girl in whose nursery the toys lived, and Sally had taken her to the nursery.

## The Poor Fairy Doll

The fairy doll was small, because the Christmas tree had been small, and she wasn't even as tall as the sailor doll. She was very beautiful. She had a mist of golden hair around her smiling face, and she wore a gauzy, frilly frock that stuck out round her. It had silver stars on it. She had silver wings and little silver shoes. She stood on the tips of her toes and gazed round at everyone with bright blue eyes and a happy smile.

'Oh, my goodness! Here's somebody else who's always going to smile!' said the golden-haired doll, in a most disagreeable voice. She didn't like the look of the beautiful fairy doll and her shining wings.

The rag doll and the bear stared at her. They felt jealous. She looked so lovely and so new. They had seen her at the top of the Christmas tree when Sally had taken them downstairs at Christmas time. They wished *they* had been put at the top of the tree. Why should the fairy doll be tied there? She didn't belong to the nursery. She had come from a shop.

'If she thinks we are going to be friends with her just because she smiles at us in that silly way, she's making a mistake!' said the rag doll, frowning.

'If she thinks she's going to get the best place in the toy cupboard she'll find she's wrong!' said the blue rabbit.

'I don't see why she should come into the cupboard at all!' said the golden-haired doll. 'She's a stranger here. Let her stay outside.'

'Oh, please, do let me come in,' begged the fairy doll, in a fright. 'I'd be afraid to be out here all alone. Please be kind to me.'

But the toys were jealous of her and they turned her out of the toy cupboard, and told her to go and sleep in the coal scuttle.

'Go on!' said the rag doll unkindly. 'You will find it quite comfortable!'

Well, the fairy doll really believed her, and so she went to the coal scuttle. She climbed on to the top of the coal and tried to settle down comfortably. But of course she couldn't. She began to cry, for she felt very lonely and tired.

Then she found that her beautiful gauzy frock was all dirty! Her pink legs were dirty! Her silver shoes were dirty! She rubbed her eyes and looked down at herself in dismay.

'Oh! My beautiful clothes are ruined!' she sobbed.

She did look strange. She had rubbed her tear-stained face and made dark streaks all

4

*'Oh, please, do let me come in.'*

down it. She climbed out of the coal scuttle, sad and puzzled, for she still did not know that it was the coal that had made her so dirty.

Now the sailor doll had been left downstairs, for Sally had taken him down to the dining-room. As soon as the house was quiet and everyone was asleep, the sailor got up from the chair where Sally had put him, and stretched himself.

'I shan't stay down here,' he thought. 'It's dull. I'll go up to the nursery. But I must remember not to sing, or else the toys will be angry with me.'

So the little sailor doll jumped down from the chair and ran to the door. He climbed up the stairs, humming softly to himself. When he got to the nursery he was surprised to hear the sound of crying. He stood still and looked round to see who it was.

Nearby, her face tearful, her hands and legs dirty and her lovely frock spoilt, stood the fairy doll. She was crying bitterly. The sailor stared at her. She looked really dreadful, not a bit pretty, and her lovely smile was all gone.

'What's the matter?' asked the sailor doll, in his deep, kind voice. The fairy doll looked at him through her tears. He was smiling as usual.

It was the first time that anyone had smiled at the fairy doll and she felt very grateful.

'Oh,' she said, 'the toys wouldn't let me sleep in the toy cupboard with them. They told me to go and sleep in the coal scuttle. So I did. I didn't know it would make me all dirty like this. What am I to do?'

The sailor doll was kind. He took her hand. 'At first I wasn't sure who you were,' he said. 'But now I see that you are the fairy doll from the top of the Christmas tree. How very unkind of the toys to make you get into the coal scuttle! Come with me. I can get a bowl of water and some soap, and maybe we can clean you up. You really do look dreadful.'

The sailor doll climbed up to the basin and turned on a tap. He filled a little dish with warm water. He broke a bit off the soap in the basin and put it into his dish. Then he climbed down again. He washed the fairy doll's hands for her, and her face and legs. She came pink and clean again, and her smile came back.

'You have a lovely smile,' said the sailor doll, looking at her. 'Nobody smiles in this nursery, not even the pink cat.'

'*You* have a nice smile, too,' said the doll shyly. 'I like it.'

'Do you really?' said the sailor joyfully. 'I'm so glad. Nobody else likes it. They don't like my song either.'

'Oh, have you got a song?' said the fairy doll, delighted. 'Songs are lovely. Sing it to me.'

So the sailor sang his song to her. You know how it went:

*'Yoho for a life on the sea,*
*Yoho, that's the life for me!*
*I wish I'd a ship*
*For I'd take a long trip,*
*Yoho for a life on the sea!*
*YOHO!'*

The fairy doll listened. 'That's the nicest song I ever heard,' she said. 'I specially like the loud YOHO at the end.'

'Do you really?' said the sailor, smiling all over his face. 'All the others hate it.'

As he spoke, he saw the rag doll, the teddy bear, the blue rabbit, the pink cat and the golden-haired doll coming over to him, looking very cross indeed.

'Will you stop that awful noise?' said the rag doll quite fiercely.

'The fairy doll likes it,' said the sailor. 'I'm singing it to her, not to you.'

'Well, I'm surprised you want even to *talk* to

such a dirty little creature!' said the golden-haired doll, turning up her nose at the fairy doll.

'And whose fault is it that she's dirty?' cried the sailor doll. 'It's yours, you unkind things! She's a dear, smiling little doll, and you've treated her most unfairly.'

'Well, we don't like her and we shall go on treating her just as we please,' said the teddy bear.'

'I don't want to stay in this nursery,' sobbed the fairy doll. 'I'll go away.'

'Then I shall come with you,' said the sailor doll at once, putting his arm round the fairy doll. 'We'll go to Toyland! I don't know the way, but we'll get there somehow. The people there couldn't be more unkind than the toys here. Goodbye, Toys! You won't see us any more!'

And with that the sailor doll took off his cap politely, bowed to the surprised toys and walked out of the door with the fairy doll.

That was the beginning of their adventures. What an exciting time they are going to have!

# Off to Toyland

The sailor doll went down the stairs with the fairy doll. She clung to his hand, for she was frightened. She didn't know where Toyland was, she didn't know how to get there and she didn't know how long it would take—all she knew was that she had found a friend who smiled at her.

'That makes me happy, although I feel sad whenever I see my dirty frock and shoes,' said the fairy doll to herself. The sailor took her into the garden. It was a moonlit night and the moon swam in and out of the little clouds.

'Come along,' said the sailor doll kindly. 'What is your name? Have you got one?'

'Not really,' said the fairy doll. 'Nobody ever calls me anything but Fairy doll. But I'd like to have a name.'

'Would you?' said the sailor doll, looking at her. 'Well, shall I choose one for you—or would you like to choose your own?'

'*You* choose,' said the fairy doll shyly.

'Well, I shall call you Tiptoe,' said the sailor doll, 'because you walk on tiptoe. Now you choose a name for me, because I haven't a name either.'

'I think I'd rather like to call you Jolly,' said the fairy doll, 'because you *are* so smiley and jolly.'

'That's a lovely name, Tiptoe,' said the sailor, pleased. 'I do like it. Tiptoe and Jolly—they sound nice, don't they? Now come along. We'll never get to Toyland if we don't hurry!'

Soon they met a hedgehog scurrying along in the moonlight as if he were a clockwork animal. Tiptoe gave a scream. Jolly put her behind him, for he was not quite sure what this hurrying creature was.

'Hello!' said the hedgehog, surprised. 'Toys out at night! Well, I never! I suppose you haven't seen any snails, slugs, caterpillars, grubs, or beetles, have you?'

'No,' said Jolly, in astonishment. 'What do you want those for?'

'For my supper!' said the hedgehog. 'Well, goodbye.'

'Wait a minute!' called the sailor doll, hurrying after him. 'Wait a minute. Can you tell us the way to Toyland, please?'

'Didn't know there was such a place!' said the hedgehog, and disappeared under a bush.

Jolly was disappointed. Never mind, maybe they would find someone else to ask. And, sure enough, in another minute they heard the pitter-patter of a field mouse's little feet.

'Hi, Mouse!' called the sailor doll. 'Half a minute!'

'What's the matter?' asked the mouse, stopping. 'Who are you? You're not mice or hedgehogs or spiders or rabbits or rats or any of the creatures I know. What do you want? Don't you dare to try and eat me!'

'Of course not!' said the sailor doll, laughing. 'We are toys and want to know the way to Toyland. Can you tell us?'

'No, but I can tell you the way to Mouse-land,' said the mouse, pulling at his long whiskers. 'You take the first turn to the left by that snowdrop—then to the right by a lilac bush, then . . .'

'Thank you,' said Jolly. 'But we don't want to go to Mouseland. Goodbye!'

They went through the hedge at the bottom of the garden and came out into a field. A large sandy rabbit was very startled to see them. He was just about to spring back into his hole when Jolly called to him.

'Hi, Bunny! Tell us the way to Toyland.'

'Is that where Father Christmas lives?' asked the rabbit, popping his head out of his hole.

'I don't know,' said the sailor doll. He had never heard of Father Christmas. But Tiptoe had, because she had been on the top of a Christmas tree at Christmas time, and she knew all about him. She had heard the children talking.

'Yes, I think he *must* live in Toyland,' she said, 'because he brings so many toys.'

'Well, listen,' said the rabbit, his big eyes shining like glass in the moonlight. 'There's a brownie who lives in the wood over there, in an oak tree. He knows Father Christmas. He might be able to tell you where Toyland is.'

'Thank you,' said Jolly gratefully. He took Tiptoe's hand and they set off to the wood. When they got there they called loudly, 'Brownie! Brownie! Where are you?'

A voice answered from the middle of the wood. 'Coming! Who wants me?'

'Jolly and Tiptoe want you!' shouted back the two dolls, and in about two minutes they heard the sound of someone coming through the bushes. It was a bright-eyed brownie with a shining beard. 'What do you want?' he asked.

13

'We want to ask you the way to Toyland,' said Jolly.

'Why, are you toys?' asked the brownie. '*She* doesn't look like a toy. She looks like a fairy.'

'Well, she's not,' said Jolly. 'She's a doll. Please tell us the way, Brownie. We're getting cold. Is it very far?'

'It is, rather,' said the brownie. 'You'd better go by train.'

'Oh, that would be lovely!' said Tiptoe. 'Do you mean the kind of train that real children go in?'

'Of course not,' said the brownie. 'Go down that rabbit hole and you'll come to a station. Take tickets for Toyland and get into the train when it comes along.'

'Oh, thank you,' said the dolls and they ran towards the rabbit hole, feeling really excited. The brownie yelled after them, 'Give my love to Father Christmas. Don't forget now!'

Tiptoe and Jolly went down the dark rabbit hole. It led down and down for a long way and twisted about a good deal. Then suddenly it opened out into a little underground station, where yellow rails ran beside a little platform. There was a ticket office at the end. Jolly went up to it.

'Two tickets for Toyland, please,' he said.
'I hope they don't cost anything, for I've no
money.'

'Well, in that case you'll have to have them
for nothing,' said the ticket man. He was a
round, cute little fellow who kept yawning all
the time. 'Take the next train. Don't change
anywhere. Get out at Toyland Station, go up
the steps and you'll see Toyland Gates. Here
are your tickets.'

No sooner had they taken their tickets than
the train rumbled in. It was almost exactly like
a wooden toy train, with open carriages. It was
very full of elves, brownies, fairies, rabbits,
moles and other creatures. Jolly and Tiptoe
squeezed themselves in beside a brownie and a
mole. There was more room in another carriage,
but a hedgehog was curled up there and Jolly
thought he was too prickly to sit next to.

The train went off. It rumbled through
underground passages lit by lamps and stopped
at all kinds of interesting stations.

At Cheese Town all the mice got out. At
Lettuce Corner all the rabbits jumped down to
the platform. At Elf Town the fairy folk got
down—and by the time that 'Toyland' was
reached, only the two dolls were left in the

train. The driver leaned out and called to them, 'Here you are, Toys! Get out here!'

They got out, rather excited, went up the long flight of steps and came out into the open air. Not far off were two huge wooden gates and across them was written in big red letters:

ENTRANCE TO TOYLAND

'We're there!' cried Jolly, and he gave Tiptoe a kiss. 'At last!'

But nobody opened the gates to them. Instead a little man popped out of a small round house nearby and called to them. 'Hi, do you want to go in? Well, you can't unless you're toys.'

'We *are* toys!' said Jolly.

'*She's* not!' said the little man. 'She's a fairy. Look at her dress and her wings—and her wand too. She can't go to Toyland. Only toys live there.'

'Now look here, I tell you she's a doll,' said Jolly crossly. But the little man simply would *not* believe them, and he went into his round house and banged the door. Jolly stared miserably at poor Tiptoe.

'Isn't that dreadful!' he said. 'Fancy getting right to the gates of Toyland and not getting in!'

Tiptoe wept bitterly. 'You'd better go in by yourself and leave me here,' she sobbed.

*Entrance to Toyland*

'As if I would do a thing like that!' said Jolly.

As Tiptoe was crying, somebody came walking by. It was a little woman carrying a washing basket. She stopped and looked at Tiptoe.

'What's the matter?' she asked. Jolly told her. The washer-woman took the fairy doll's hand and squeezed it.

'Don't you worry,' she said. 'You come home with me and I'll fix up something for you. You don't want that dirty fairy frock any more, do you? Well, leave it with me, and I'll wash it and use it for something or other—it would make pretty curtains for my windows. And I'll give you one of my overalls instead. Then you won't look like a fairy. You wait there whilst I take the washing to the round house.'

The two dolls watched the washer-woman deliver her washing basket at the round house where the cross little gate-keeper lived. Then they went with the kind old woman back to her cottage.

She made the fairy doll take off her frilly frock and she popped it into a wash tub. She made her take off her dirty silver shoes and gave them to the sailor, to clean.

'Now you just pop into bed for a little while,'

she said to Tiptoe. 'When you wake up, you'll find that everything is all right. You'll be able to get into Toyland as easily as can be!'

So Tiptoe popped into bed and went to sleep. Jolly cleaned her shoes and sang his song to the washer-woman. And the washer-woman listened with delight and altered one of her red-flowered overalls for Tiptoe.

'Things will soon be all right!' she said. 'You just see!'

# Toyland at Last!

When Tiptoe, the fairy doll woke up, she found that the kind old washer-woman had altered the red overall very nicely indeed. It lay on the end of the bed looking very pretty. Tiptoe stood up in her petticoat and put on the overall. It fitted her beautifully.

She went into the kitchen. 'What shall I do about my wings?' she asked. 'You haven't made holes for them to come out of the overall, Washer-woman.'

'I know,' said the old dame. 'But if you keep your wings hidden you will look less than ever like a fairy. Keep them under your overall. Now tell me—what are you going to do when you get to Toyland?'

'I don't really know,' said Jolly, his smiling face looking rather worried. 'I hadn't thought about that. We must get a little house to live in. I think really we had better get married. That would be fun. Then you could always darn my socks, Tiptoe, and I could always look after you.'

'I should like that,' said Tiptoe, smiling at the jolly little sailor doll. 'You are always so cheerful and happy, and so am I when people are kind to me. We should get on well together.'

'Then we will get married and find a dear little house to live in!' said the sailor joyfully. The washer-woman shook her head.

'Toyland is very, very crowded,' she said. 'I don't believe there is a single empty house. What will you do then?'

'We'll think about that when we get there,' said Jolly. 'Now what about starting off? Thank you, Washer-woman, for all you have done for us. Doesn't Tiptoe look sweet?'

'She does,' said the old woman, smiling at the doll in the red overall, her golden hair like a mist round her head. 'Be careful that a clown or a teddy bear doesn't run off with her, Sailor.'

'Oh, don't say things like that!' squealed Tiptoe. 'I don't like clowns, or bears. They haven't been kind to me.'

'*I'll* look after you!' said Jolly. 'Come along now. We must go!'

So off they went—and this time the gate-keeper didn't say that Tiptoe was a fairy. He didn't even know she was the same doll that he had refused to let into Toyland! He swung the big gates open wide and the two dolls walked in.

Toyland was lovely. There were all kinds of dolls' houses everywhere, set in proper streets. Some were big and some were small. There were shops too, especially sweet shops. There were farms here and there, with dozens of toy animals in them, walking about, or drinking at the little streams and ponds. Toy ducks swam merrily on the water and toy dogs barked at toy sheep.

'This is lovely,' said Jolly, pleased. 'Isn't it nice to be in Toyland, Tiptoe? We shall be very happy here.'

'We must look for an empty house,' said Tiptoe, slipping her little hand into Jolly's. 'We must have somewhere to live.'

So they wandered up and down the streets of Toyland looking for an empty house. But there wasn't one anywhere! It was most disappointing.

'What *are* we going to do?' said Jolly, his smile almost disappearing off his jolly face. He saw a toy policeman stopping the traffic in the market-square and hurried up to him.

'We can't find an empty house,' he said. 'What shall we do?'

'Build one!' said the policeman waving the traffic on. 'Go to the warehouse where toy bricks are stored and choose what you want.'

The dolls hurried to where he pointed. They came to a big building and when they went inside they found that there were great boxes of toy bricks there, some all arranged to build a house, some to build farms, and others to build forts. There was a picture on the front of each box to show what the finished house or farm would look like.

Tiptoe and Jolly chose a box whose picture showed a dear little cottage with two rooms, a tall chimney and pretty windows. They asked if they might take away the box and the shopman said yes.

He lent them a big wooden cart to take away the box. Off they went with their box of house bricks to look for a place to build.

Soon they came to a pleasant sunny hillside, with a little pond at the bottom and a stream running merrily down the hill.

'This would be a lovely place for our house,' said Tiptoe.

'So it would,' said Jolly. He opened the lid of the big box, and soon he and Tiptoe were pulling out the bricks. There was a little book that told them exactly how to build the house. I expect you would know how to build one, because you must often have built all kinds of toy houses with your bricks.

Soon the walls were built. Openings were left to put the little glass windows in. Then the roof was put on and the chimney was fitted in.

'Isn't it beginning to look perfectly lovely!' cried Tiptoe in delight.

It took them two days to build the house. They slept under a haystack at night. They would have finished the house sooner, but Tiptoe put the bedroom window into the kitchen wall by mistake and it had to be taken out again.

'Now it's really finished!' cried Jolly at last. 'What about furniture, Tiptoe?'

'We'll go and buy some at a shop,' said Tiptoe. 'We haven't any money but perhaps they will let us have the furniture without any, or we can promise to pay them when we get some.'

They went to a furniture shop. They found that the furniture was sold in boxes, just as the bricks were. The shopman opened box after box to show them what kind of furniture was inside. They chose three boxes.

*Building the house*

One box had all bedroom furniture with a really nice little wardrobe and a very fine bed, besides lots of other things. The second box had kitchen tables and chairs. And the third box had a kitchen stove and a nice fireplace in it. The two dolls took the boxes home in great delight.

They soon arranged all the new furniture in their little house. It fitted beautifully. The stove went into a corner and Tiptoe got it going at once, to see if it would really cook. And it did.

Jolly moved in the bedroom furniture. The wardrobe was very difficult to get through the door. 'It's a good thing there are no stairs in our house,' said Jolly. 'I could never have got it up. Oh, look, Tiptoe — there is such a lot of room in the wardrobe to hang coats and frocks.'

'Well, we haven't any other clothes except those we are wearing,' said Tiptoe. 'But it will be nice to have a wardrobe to put things into when we *do* get them!'

'I will earn a lot of money and buy you heaps of pretty frocks,' said Jolly. 'I am a sailor, you know, and I will soon get a ship to sail, and then I will bring a lot of money home to you.'

'Oh, don't sail away and leave me!' cried Tiptoe in alarm. 'I have got so used to your nice

smiling face by now and I do love your yoho
song so much. Don't leave me!'

'I won't leave you yet,' promised Jolly. 'Now
just come and look at the bedroom, Tiptoe.
Isn't it sweet?'

Well, you should have seen that dear little
house when it was finished! It looked so neat
and pretty. Tiptoe opened the windows to let
in the sun. She lit a fire in the fireplace and
smoke came out of the chimney. It was all most
exciting.

'What shall we call our house, Jolly?' asked
Tiptoe, standing at the door with him and
looking down the hill.

'We'll call it "Jolly Cottage",' said Jolly. 'That
sounds a nice name, because we always will be
jolly in it.'

So it was called 'Jolly Cottage' and that very
day, Jolly the sailor doll and Tiptoe the fairy
doll began to live there happily.

# Tiptoe and Jolly Give a Party

Tiptoe and Jolly lived happily in 'Jolly Cottage' together. They had a family of wooden soldiers living in a house on one side of them and a clockwork clown on the other. They liked the clown very much because he did such funny things.

He didn't walk down the hill to the town as Tiptoe and Jolly did. He went head-over-heels as fast as anything. It was great fun to watch him.

When Tiptoe saw him coming out of his little house she would call to Jolly at once. 'Jolly! Jolly, do come quickly! The clown is just going shopping!'

Then they would both stand at the window and watch the clown going head-over-heels down the hill to do his shopping. Once Jolly tried to do it, but he didn't look where he was going and landed in the pond. Tiptoe had to take all his clothes and dry them by the fire. He sat in his pyjamas till they were dry.

The wooden soldiers used to march down the hill in a straight line to do their shopping. It was quite fun to watch them too. The Captain was very strict with them and if any soldier got out of line he would shout at him very fiercely and wave his sword.

'Tiptoe, I think we ought to give a party,' said Jolly one day. 'We ought to get to know everyone. It would be fun. Let's ask the clown and the soldiers to start with.'

'Oooh, yes,' said Tiptoe. 'And let's ask Mr To-and-Fro. I love the way he wobbles about.'

Mr To-and-Fro was a funny man with no legs. He got about by wobbling to and fro. He always boasted that nobody could knock him down and Jolly always longed to try, but didn't quite like to.

'And we'll ask the big toy duck that quacks so politely every time we meet him,' said Jolly. 'And what about the bunny with the pink ribbon? He's really rather a dear.'

'Yes, he lives in a little treehouse with a doll called Josie and a clockwork mouse called Click,' said Tiptoe. 'We'll ask them all!'

So Jolly got some invitation cards and wrote them to the wooden soldiers, the clockwork clown, Mr To-and-Fro, the toy duck, and Josie,

Click, and Bun. Tiptoe went out to leave them at the houses. She felt excited and important. It was simply lovely to be giving a party.

'We will give them egg sandwiches because everybody likes those,' said Jolly.

'And creamy milk,' said Tiptoe. 'And I'll make some buns with cherries on the top. My little stove will cook them beautifully.'

When the day of the party came, Tiptoe went to pick some flowers for her vases. Then she put on an apron and made three dishes of little buns with cherries on the top. They did look nice.

The guests were coming at four o'clock — and do you know, at half-past three, when Tiptoe wanted to make the egg sandwiches and pour creamy milk into her little blue cups, she found that the eggs and the milk hadn't come!

'Jolly!' she cried. 'Where are the eggs and milk? Didn't you get them?'

'Of course not,' said Jolly. 'I thought *you* were going to get them! Oh, goodness, *now* what are we to do?'

'You must hurry to the shops and buy some, quickly,' said Tiptoe. 'Oh dear, oh dear — our first party and we have only got cherry buns!'

'Tiptoe, it's Wednesday and the shops are

shut,' said Jolly in a very small voice, his wide smile almost gone from his face.

'Jolly! What in the world are we to do?' cried Tiptoe. She went to the window and looked out to see if any of her guests were coming. Yes— here was Mr To-and-Fro wobbling to and fro up the hill. She ran to meet him.

'Oh, Mr To-and-Fro, I'm so pleased to see you, but it's going to be a dreadful party, because the eggs haven't come for the egg sandwiches and the milk hasn't come for you all to drink. Whatever can we do?'

'Dear me!' said Mr To-and-Fro, standing quite straight and looking upset. 'That's very serious. You really *must* have sandwiches at a party—and of course your guests must have something to drink. Let me think. I'm good at thinking. So just let me think.'

Tiptoe stood still and let Mr To-and-Fro think hard. He began to wobble a little and then he smiled all round his funny wooden head.

'Dear little Tiptoe, I've such a good idea. You know the farm on the other side of the hill? Well, a very nice cow lives there, called Mrs Buttercup—oh, a very charming cow with most beautiful manners. And a fine little red hen lives there too, with her friends. They are called Mrs Cluck, Mrs Cackle and Mrs Squawk. Now what about asking them to the party? If you do, they are sure to offer you milk and eggs.'

'Oh, what a marvellous idea!' cried Tiptoe in delight. 'Mr To-and-Fro, do go and ask them for me. I've seen them so often and I like them very much. I'd have asked them to my party, but I didn't somehow think of asking a cow and hens.'

Mr To-and-Fro wobbled off over the top of the hill. He soon came back with Mrs Buttercup, the pretty wooden cow, and the three toy hens, all most excited and pleased. Mrs Buttercup had put a blue ribbon round her neck and a little bell that tinkled as she walked. The hens had pink ribbons round their waists. Mrs Cluck put out her foot and shook hands with Tiptoe and Jolly.

'It's *so* kind of you to ask us to your party,' she clucked. 'Mr To-and-Fro tells us that you haven't got any eggs or milk. Well, we shall each of us be very pleased to lay you an egg and Mrs Buttercup can give you plenty of milk.'

'How kind of you!' cried Tiptoe, delighted. 'Do go into the kitchen and lay your eggs there, then I can boil them quickly and make my sandwiches. And, Mrs Buttercup, Jolly could milk you if you don't mind standing still where you are.'

Well, in a short time there were three eggs on the woolly rug in front of the fire and Jolly brought in a can of frothy warm milk from kind Mrs Buttercup. In a trice the blue cups were filled and Tiptoe cut four plates of egg sandwiches. The party was ready to begin!

All the other guests arrived in a bunch. The wooden soldiers saluted Tiptoe in rather a grand manner. The clockwork clown bowed very low and then went head-over-heels round the kitchen. The toy duck, whose name was Quack, opened his beak and quacked so excitedly that Tiptoe could hardly understand what he said. Josie, Click and Bun shook hands and smiled all round. They always loved a party.

They all ate a very good tea, and everyone told Mrs Cluck, Mrs Cackle and Mrs Squawk that the egg in the egg sandwiches was the most delicious they had ever tasted. And when Jolly said that the milk was the creamiest he had ever had in his life, Mrs Buttercup blushed red all over with delight. Instead of being a red and white cow, she suddenly looked a red cow and everyone stared at her in surprise. But she soon went back to red and white again.

They played a fine lot of games. One game was trying to push Mr To-and-Fro over. Everyone had a turn.

'If anyone pushes me right over on the ground so that I have to stay there, I will give them a silver coin!' said Mr To-and-Fro. So you should have seen the soldiers pushing him with all their might. But he only wobbled to and fro, to and fro, because, you see, he had a heavy weight at the bottom of him so that he couldn't possibly fall over even if he wanted to. He had to go to sleep standing up at night, because he couldn't even lie down.

Then the soldiers did some splendid marching up and down and round about, and everyone clapped. Then they all played hunt-the-thimble and suddenly, the thimble was lost.

It had been put on Quack's yellow beak—and he had sneezed and swallowed the thimble!

'I'm dreadfully, dreadfully sorry,' he quacked. 'Oh dear—and now I've got the hiccups! Do pardon me!'

But nobody minded that, because in the middle of a hiccup the thimble came back. Quack was so glad.

'It's been a lovely party,' said Josie, at last.

*The soldiers did some splendid marching.*

'We're so glad you came to Toyland, Tiptoe and Jolly. Do come and see us sometime. Please excuse us if we go now, but Click is yawning and as he's only a baby mouse, I must take him home to bed.'

Then one by one everyone went. Mrs Butter-cup mooed her thanks, and said that she would always be pleased to let Tiptoe and Jolly have milk at any time. Mr To-and-Fro wobbled so quickly down the hill that he nearly went into the pond. The soldiers saluted and went home. The clockwork clown said he would stay behind and help to clear up. Quack kissed Tiptoe with his big yellow beak and went off happily with the three cackling hens.

'What a marvellous party!' said Tiptoe, beginning to wash up. 'It's so nice to think we've made friends with such a lot of people.'

'I'll dry the dishes for you,' said the clock-work clown. 'Jolly, you'd better sweep up the bits on the carpet. And I say—what about you coming and having supper with me? I've got a nice big chocolate cake and some coffee.'

Well, that was a lovely end to a lovely day. The clockwork clown took them back to his cottage and they ate chocolate cake and drank coffee till they were too sleepy to talk. Then they said goodnight and went back to 'Jolly Cottage'. They snuggled into bed and tucked themselves up well.

'I'm so glad we came to Toyland,' said Tiptoe sleepily.

'So am I,' said Jolly. 'Let's talk about our party, Tiptoe.' But they couldn't, because they were both fast asleep!

## The Unlucky Clockwork Clown

One day Tiptoe went out to do some shopping by herself. Jolly was planting roses to grow round the cottage. Tiptoe took her basket and set off, humming a little tune.

On the way a great cloud blew up and down came the rain. Good gracious! Poor Tiptoe was in a bad way because she only had on her red overall—no coat at all!

Just as she was wondering where she could shelter, up ran the clockwork clown. He had a small green umbrella and he offered it to Tiptoe at once.

'Oh, but you'll get wet,' said Tiptoe.

'That doesn't matter,' said the clown. 'Pray take my umbrella. I can't bear to see you getting wet. You can give it back to me tomorrow. I am going shopping.'

Well, Tiptoe was very glad of the umbrella. She went home up the hill and the little green umbrella kept her nice and dry. Jolly was looking out for her very anxiously.

'What a nice umbrella!' he said. 'Where did you get it?'

'The clown lent it to me,' said Tiptoe. 'Wasn't it nice of him? I do hope he won't get very wet. He was going shopping. I think I will go and stand his umbrella by his front door, then he will see it when he comes home.'

So she did, and then she went back to cook the dinner on her little stove.

Tiptoe and Jolly didn't see the clockwork clown that day. They looked out for him the next day, but they didn't see him then either. When the third day came and he didn't appear, they really felt very worried.

'I'm going to see if he's all right,' said Tiptoe at last. 'You come with me, Jolly.' So they both went to the little house next door and knocked loudly.

A very small, weak voice called out 'Come in!' So in they went. And there was the poor clockwork clown in bed, looking very sorry for himself.

'Are you ill?' asked Tiptoe, running to him.

'No,' said the clockwork clown. 'I did have a chill the day before yesterday when I was caught in the rain, so I went to bed. But yesterday I felt quite all right and I wanted to get up. But I can't wind myself up. Something's gone wrong with my key—and I'm s-s-s-s-soooooooo unhappy!'

He burst into tears. Jolly made him sit up and he looked at the clown's back, where there was usually a key sticking out. The clockwork clown could reach this quite easily to wind himself up when he ran down. He couldn't walk or run or turn head-over-heels unless he was wound up each day.

'Good gracious! Haven't you been able to get out of bed because you weren't wound up?' cried Jolly.

'N-n-n-n-nooooo!' wept the clown.

'So you haven't been able to get yourself anything to eat!' cried Tiptoe, almost crying herself, because she felt so sorry for the poor clown.

'N-n-n-n-nooooo!' sobbed the clown, making the sheet all wet with his tears.

'*I'll* soon put you right!' said Jolly, and he took hold of the key. But he couldn't turn it. He tried and he tried.

'*I've* tried hundreds of times but it's no good,' said the clown.

Jolly took the key out and looked at it. 'It's all gone rusty!' he said.

*'It's gone all rusty!'*

'Has it?' said the clown. 'Well, it must have got wet in the rain that day when I lent Tiptoe my umbrella. Things go rusty if they get wet, don't they? Oh dear, oh dear—now I can never be wound up again!'

'Now don't cry any more,' said Jolly, putting the rusty key into his pocket. 'I'll go and find another key for you somewhere. Cheer up! Tiptoe will get you some bread and milk, and look after you. I suppose you'll have to stay in bed till we find another key to wind you up.'

Tiptoe began to make some bread and milk. The clown wiped his eyes with the sheet and waited. He was dreadfully hungry. Jolly went out feeling certain he could get another key quickly.

'Poor old clown!' he thought. 'He did a kind deed and lent Tiptoe his umbrella, and got his key all rusty. That wasn't a very good reward. I'll see what I can do for him.'

Jolly went to the town. He asked the toy policeman in the market square if he knew where he could get a key for the clown.

'You'd better go to the police station,' said the policeman. 'All lost keys are taken there and if they are not claimed, they go into a big box. Then if anyone needs a new key they can see if one of those fits them.'

Jolly went to the little toy police station. A big clockwork policeman looked up as he went in. He kept putting his hand up and down, and this puzzled Jolly at first.

'Why do you do that?' he asked. 'Are you saluting me?'

'No,' said the policeman. 'I have to do this when I am directing the traffic, so when I am just sitting here I still have to do it, because my arm goes by clockwork. It will run down in a minute, then I'll be all right.'

Jolly waited till the policeman's arm had stopped working. Then he took out the rusty key from his pocket. 'Have you a key this size?' he asked.

The policeman went to a big box and opened it. It was full of keys from clockwork toys. He spread them out on a table and he and Jolly sorted them out. But they simply could *not* find one that was just the same size.

'No good,' said the policeman. 'I'm sorry. The clown won't be able to be wound up any more.'

'But that's dreadful,' said Jolly, in dismay, thinking of the many times he had seen the clown going head-over-heels down the hill. 'Oh, whatever shall I do?'

He left the police station and walked down the street. He was thinking so hard that he didn't see where he was going and he walked straight into Josie, Click and Bun.

'Hello, Jolly!' they cried. 'Look out! You nearly knocked us over! What's the matter? You do look gloomy.'

Jolly told them. He showed them the rusty key. 'Oh!' cried Click, 'the same thing happened to me once. But I got another key, look!'

'Where did you get it?' asked Jolly. 'I've been to the police station and looked at all the lost keys. There aren't any the right size.'

'We got Click's at the clock shop,' said Josie. 'The only thing is, it's the key belonging to an old chiming clock, so Click chimes at every hour. Listen—it's just about the hour now.'

They all stood and listened—and sure enough, Click suddenly chimed. 'Ding-dong-ding-dong!' he went. 'Ding-dong-ding-dong!' It *was* funny to hear him.

'I'll go to the clock shop,' said Jolly cheerfully. So all four of them went along. But the clock-work clown's key was rather a large one and there wasn't a single clock key that would do.

'Anyway, I'm sure he wouldn't like to chime the hour or strike like a clock,' said Jolly.

44

'Really, this is very sad. I simply don't know what to do. I hate going back to tell the clown that he'll never be wound up again.'

He said a sad goodbye to Josie, Click and Bun, and went up the hill. On the way he met the Captain of the wooden soldiers. The Captain waved his sword at Jolly. It gleamed brightly in the sunshine.

'What's up, my friend?' cried the Captain. 'You look as sad as a hen left out in the rain.'

'That's just about what I feel like,' said Jolly sadly, and he told the Captain of the soldiers all about the rusty key and the poor clockwork clown who would never be able to walk, or run, or turn head-over-heels again.

'Bless us all!' cried the Captain, taking the key. 'Why didn't you come and tell *me*? I can put this right for you in two shakes of a duck's tail. Half a minute—I'll be back!'

Before the sailor doll could ask him anything, he had snatched the key from his hand and run to his house. Jolly heard him shouting loud commands. He stood and stared in surprise.

'What in the world does he think he can do to put things right?' he wondered. 'They are not clockwork soldiers. They are wooden. They have no keys at all!'

In about half a minute the Captain came out of his house—and in his hand he carried the clown's key. But you should just have seen it now! It shone like silver! It winked in the sun like a live thing. It was as bright and clean as the Captain's own shining sword!

'There you are, my boy!' said the Captain, handing Jolly the key. 'Easy as could be! My men have to shine up my sword each day and see that it doesn't get rusty, and they have to clean their guns too, and their buttons. So it was easy to make them get the rust off this key for you. I think you'll find that it winds up the clown easily now.'

Jolly thanked him joyfully and flew to the clown's cottage. He burst in at the door so suddenly that he made the clown upset his bread and milk all over the bed.

He stuck the shining key into the clown's back and turned it. 'Ur-r-r-r-r-r, Ur-r-r-r-r,' went the key, and wound up the clown as easily as anything. The clown jumped out of bed and turned head-over-heels seven times all round the room. Over and over he went, and made Tiptoe laugh so much that she got a stitch in her side.

'Where did you get my lovely new key?' asked the clown at last.

'It isn't new, it's the same one,' said Jolly, and he told the clown all about it. The clown grinned all over his face.

'Good old Captain of the soldiers!' he said. 'I'm going to thank him this very minute.' And off he went, turning head-over-heels faster than ever. The soldiers were on the hillside, being drilled—and the clown knocked them all over like skittles, because he couldn't stop.

But nobody minded. They were all so pleased to see the dear old clown himself again. It really was a good thing, wasn't it!

# *Where Has Jolly Gone?*

Now once Mr To-and-Fro, the wobbly man, had a birthday coming. He didn't always remember his birthday, but this year he did, and he thought it would be a fine idea to give a birthday party.

'I really must ask those two nice dolls, Tiptoe and Jolly,' he thought. 'I'm not going to bother to write invitation cards. I'll just go round and ask everybody I can think of.'

So he set off, wobbling down the street. He met Bruiny the teddy bear, and he asked him. He met the pink cat and asked her, and he met the Skittle family of nine, and asked all of them too.

'Gracious!' said the skittles, who always said exactly the same things at exactly the same moment. 'Gracious! Do you want us *all* to come! Thank you very much! We hope you will have room in your house for everyone!'

Mr To-and-Fro wobbled up the hill to where the soldiers, the clockwork clown, and Tiptoe and Jolly lived. Everyone was most excited, especially Tiptoe, who loved a party better than anything else in the world.

But after Mr To-and-Fro had gone wobbling off down the hill, Jolly noticed that Tiptoe was very quiet.

'What's the matter, Tiptoe?' he asked. 'Are you feeling ill?'

'No, I'm quite well, thank you,' said Tiptoe, but she didn't smile at all.

Jolly watched her for a little while and then he went and put his arms round her. 'There *is* something the matter,' he said. 'Please tell me, dear Tiptoe.'

'Oh, it's nothing,' said Tiptoe, and she ran into the bedroom. 'I'm going to make the bed,' she said.

She seemed to be a very long time making the bed and soon, Jolly peeped in at the door to see what she was doing. And, dear me, she was sitting on the little bedroom chair crying as if her heart would break! Tears dripped out from between her pink fingers and made a little puddle on the floor.

Jolly was most alarmed, for Tiptoe hardly ever cried. She was a very smiley doll indeed. He ran to her and hugged her.

'Tiptoe! You must be ill! Go to bed and I will get the doctor.'

'I'm not ill,' said Tiptoe. 'I'm only sad, that's all.'

'But why?' cried Jolly, in surprise. 'Have *I* done anything to make you sad?'

'Oh no,' said Tiptoe. 'But oh, Jolly—you know Mr To-and-Fro asked us to his birthday party. Well, I c-c-c-can't g-g-g-go!' And poor Tiptoe put her head into her hands again and wept two such large tears that they made quite a splash when they fell on the floor.

'But *why* can't you go?' cried Jolly, feeling more and more puzzled.

'Because I haven't got a f-f-f-frock to go in,' sobbed Tiptoe.

'But you look very sweet in your red overall,' said Jolly.

'Oh, Jolly, don't say such *silly* things!' cried Tiptoe crossly. 'How do you think I will feel if I go to the birthday party and see Josie in a pretty frilly frock, and the skittles with bows on, and the clockwork clown in a new suit, and Bruiny in his blue sash—and I shall only be in this old red overall! Oh, I *do* feel so miserable!'

'Oh, Tiptoe, don't cry so,' said poor Jolly, feeling terribly miserable himself. 'Haven't you

'Oh, Tiptoe, don't cry so.'

anything else to go in at all?'

'Yes—there's my night-dress!' said Tiptoe, 'but how can I go in that?'

'Well, you can't very well,' said Jolly. 'Never mind, Tiptoe. If you can't go, I won't go either.'

'But I *want* you to go!' wept poor Tiptoe. 'It's bad enough that I can't go. I couldn't bear it if you didn't go either.'

Jolly got up and went into the kitchen. He made a jug of hot cocoa and took it to Tiptoe. 'Drink some of this,' he said. 'You will feel better then.'

So Tiptoe drank some. But she didn't feel any better about the party at all. She didn't smile once that day and she looked so miserable the next day, that Jolly lost his wide smile too.

'I'm just going out for a little while,' he said to Tiptoe, after dinner. 'You go and lie down, because you look tired.'

When tea-time came, Tiptoe brushed her hair and then went to put the kettle on for tea. She looked round for Jolly. But he wasn't back.

'Oh dear! I wonder where he has got to,' thought Tiptoe. She had her tea and went to the door to look for Jolly. But he was nowhere to be seen. The clockwork clown was just going by and Tiptoe called to him.

'If you see Jolly, tell him to hurry home. The tea will soon be cold in the pot.'

Six o'clock came and no Jolly. Tiptoe began to be very worried. She looked out of the door hundreds of times to see if the sailor doll was coming up the hill, but he wasn't. The wooden soldiers came by in a straight line and Tiptoe called to them, 'Have you seen Jolly? He hasn't come home to tea.'

The Captain saluted smartly. 'Yes, dear Tiptoe,' he said. 'I saw Jolly beside the river this afternoon.'

'Beside the *river*!' said Tiptoe, in astonishment. 'But that's a long way from here. Whatever was he doing there?'

'He was talking to the captain of a ship,' said the soldier, 'but I couldn't hear what they were saying. Good-day to you!'

The soldiers marched into their house. Tiptoe grew more puzzled and worried every minute. Why should Jolly go to the river and talk to the captain of a ship? He had never, never done that before. Why didn't he come home?

Josie came by with Click and Bun. They had been to tea with Mrs Buttercup, the cow over the hill. Josie waved to Tiptoe. Then she saw that she looked worried and she came over to her.

'What's the matter?' she asked.

'Jolly hasn't come home,' said Tiptoe, beginning to cry. 'The soldiers saw him talking to the captain of a ship this afternoon. Oh, why doesn't Jolly send me a message? I am so worried.'

'Did he leave a note for you?' said Josie, going indoors. 'Perhaps there is a message left in a letter on the mantelpiece.'

They looked, but there wasn't. Then Click gave a little squeal of excitement. He had been snuffling about on the rug, and he had found something in the fender.

'Here's a letter,' he said.

Tiptoe gave a cry of surprise and picked it up. 'The wind must have blown it down,' she said. 'Oh, it's a letter from Jolly.'

She opened it and read it out loud. This is what it said.

'Darling Tiptoe, I am so sorry you haven't a new dress for Mr To-and-Fro's birthday party. I am going to earn some money to get you one. Don't worry, I will soon be home again and you shall have the prettiest dress in all Toyland.

Love from
Jolly.'

'Well, if he isn't a dear!' cried Josie. 'He has gone to get some work on a ship, and that's how it was he was seen talking to a captain. Don't worry, Tiptoe. He will soon be back again.'

'I shall be so lonely all by myself till he comes back,' said Tiptoe.

'Well, if you like, Bun shall come and stay with you,' said Josie. 'Bun, would you like to stay at Jolly Cottage with Tiptoe till Jolly comes back?'

'Oh yes, please,' said the rabbit. 'I'll just go home and get my toothbrush and my pyjamas. Oh, what fun it will be!'

So Bun stayed with Tiptoe and the two of them waited until Jolly came back. They waited and they waited—and the birthday party came nearer and nearer.

'Oh, will Jolly's ship come back in time?' cried Tiptoe. 'Oh, suppose it doesn't!'

## *Jolly is a Sailor*

Jolly had been very upset because Tiptoe hadn't a party dress. After all, her red overall was getting rather old. She ought to have a party dress and look as nice as anybody else.

Jolly hadn't any money at all. So the only thing he could do was to get some work and earn some money. He set off to find a ship, for he was a sailor doll and was sure he would know how to sail one.

He went to the river that flowed in and out through Toyland. It was a nice blue river, very neat and smooth, and it had flowery banks. All kinds of toy boats, ships and steamers sailed up and down the blue water.

Jolly wandered by the river, wondering how to get some work to do. Soon he met the captain of a ship and he saluted him.

'Sir, have you any ship I can sail for you?' asked Jolly, smiling his wide smile at the captain. The captain liked him at once.

'My man, I have a ship that I want taken down to Roll-About Town,' he said. 'The trip will only take two or three days. The ship has some paint on board to paint some of the balls that live in Roll-About Town. But the ship is a sailing ship, and it *will* keep tipping over on one side, so I can't get anyone to sail it.'

Jolly knew that many toy ships do tip over on one side and lie in the water. But he felt sure he could manage the captain's ship. So he saluted again and said smartly:

'Sir Captain, I can sail your ship for you! Just try me!'

'Very well,' said the captain. 'There she is over there.'

Jolly saw a small sailing ship tied up nearby. She was painted red and blue, and had a big white sail that flapped a little in the breeze. Her name was *Saucy Sue*.

'I can sail the *Saucy Sue* for you,' said Jolly, who liked the look of the little ship very much. 'Shall I go now, sir? Is the paint aboard?'

'Yes,' said the captain. 'You may choose one man to be your crew and the two of you can sail down to Roll-About Town. Deliver the paint to Mr Bounce and then come back here. Ask for Captain Heavy-Weather and you'll soon find me. Then I'll pay you for your trouble.'

Jolly saluted and went off to the *Saucy Sue*. He wondered who he should get for his one-man crew.

'If I could get somebody very heavy, they could sit hard down when the ship heels over and their weight would make it go upright again,' he thought. 'Now who could I get?'

Just then a toy elephant went by. He was made of lead and he made a terrific noise as he went along the river bank. Clump-clump-clump went his feet. Jolly shouted to him.

'Hi, Jumbo! Do you want a job?'

'I don't think so,' said the elephant, in surprise.

'Oh, do take *this* job,' said Jolly. 'I want a one-man crew for this ship.'

'But I don't know anything about ships except that they often sink,' said the elephant, looking at the *Saucy Sue*.

'You would be the first elephant that ever sailed a ship,' said Jolly.

'Really?' said the elephant.

'And I would give you my sailor's cap to wear,' said Jolly.

'I should like that very much,' said the

elephant at once. 'I've never had a hat to wear.'

'You could only wear it whilst you were on the ship,' said Jolly. 'I should have to have it back when the trip was over.'

'Well—I *will* come if you'll give me your hat now,' said the elephant.

So Jolly gave the lead elephant his round sailor's hat and he put it on. He really did look rather grand in it. He stepped on board the *Saucy Sue* and the ship rocked dangerously.

'Hey, be careful where you tread!' shouted Jolly. 'Don't walk on the barrels of paint. Sit over there. Now, I'm going to cast off. Take hold of that rope with your trunk. Heave-ho—we're off!'

And they *were* off, sailing down the blue river, with the white sail billowing out above their heads. It was lovely.

'We're getting to a bend of the river,' said Jolly. 'The wind will be strong there. The ship may swing right over towards the left bank. Sit on the right-hand side of the ship, please, Jumbo. Then your weight will keep it upright.'

Sure enough, when the ship got to the bend, the wind caught it and it leaned right over to the left. Jumbo sat down firmly and caught hold of the rope to hold back the sail. Jolly went to sit beside Jumbo, but his light weight didn't make much difference.

'She's nearly over, she's nearly over!' yelled Jolly. 'Jumbo, lean back, lean back!'

The elephant leaned back so hard that he almost fell overboard. The *Saucy Sue* sailed safely round the bend and then swung upright again. Jolly was so thankful. His curly hair blew in the breeze and he put up his hand to pull his cap straight.

'Dear me! I forgot you're wearing my cap,' he said to Jumbo. 'You did well then. You'll know what to do the next time!'

They sailed safely down to Roll-About Town, passing Rocking Horse Village and Humming Top Town on the way. The trip took two days. They asked for Mr Bounce when they arrived and an enormous ball rolled up. He had a merry face on one side and he was very pleased to see the barrels of paint.

'Ha! Now we shall all be very cheerful!' he said. 'Is there any red? Yes! Well, I shall paint myself red one side and blue the other. Can you put the barrels on the bank, dear sailor and elephant, and if you don't mind putting them on their sides, we can roll them away so that we may paint every ball in the town!'

'She's nearly over, she's nearly over!'

All the balls of Roll-About Town came rolling up to see the ship. It really was funny to see them. They were all very jolly. Some of them bounced themselves instead of rolling, and one of them bounced right on top of the *Saucy Sue*, nearly swinging it over.

'Now, just be careful,' ordered Mr Bounce. 'You young balls must learn to behave yourselves. Goodbye, sailor and elephant! Many thanks for your help.'

The *Saucy Sue* sailed away up the river. It was very light without the barrels of paint. When it reached a specially windy corner it swung over so much that the sail almost touched the water. Jumbo sat tight—but alas, the sailor doll was hit by the swinging sail, and fell right into the river!

'Trumpeting trunks!' cried Jumbo. 'Look at that! He's gone!'

The wind swung the boat the other way and Jumbo's weight tipped it over too far. Down went the ship the other side—and Jumbo fell into the river too. What a to-do!

Goodness knows what would have happened if a family of ducks hadn't seen them and come swimming up. They were the kind of ducks you have in your bath and they bobbed up and down merrily. In a trice they pecked hold of poor Jolly and took him to the boat. It took four of them to rescue Jumbo, because he was so heavy. But at last he was back in the ship too and, wet and dripping, the two of them sailed their ship up the river again.

'Sailor,' said Jumbo, in a very small voice, 'I lost your cap when I fell into the water.'

'What a pity!' said Jolly sorrowfully. Then he gave a shout. 'Look—one of the ducks has found it!'

Sure enough, a toy duck was swimming fast after the ship with the cap on its head. Jumbo took it gratefully and put it on again, though it wasn't really very comfortable because it dripped water into his left ear.

At last they arrived back in Toy Town. Jolly tied up the *Saucy Sue* and yelled to a passing baby doll:

'Tell Captain Heavy-Weather that the *Saucy Sue* is back again, if you see him.'

In five minutes the captain came along and was delighted to hear that the paint had been taken safely to Roll-About Town. He paid Jolly a lot of money. 'You must pay your crew out of the money I give you,' he said.

So Jolly took the elephant to a hat shop and

with some of his money, he bought him a fine hat. He couldn't get him a sailor's cap, so he got him a red felt hat with a yellow feather in it. The elephant was simply overjoyed. He hurried off to show all his friends and begged Jolly to take him on the next ship he sailed in.

Then Jolly took his money to a shop that sold dresses. 'I want a dress for a pretty, smiley doll who has wings,' he said.

So the shop assistant showed him a very frilly frock with little blue bobbles sewn all over it and blue shoes to match. Jolly thought they would do beautifully for Tiptoe. He had them packed into a box and then he set off home.

'Ha, Tiptoe!' he thought joyfully. 'What a fine surprise you will have!'

## Mr To-and-Fro's
## Birthday Party

Now, the very day of the party came and still there was no Jolly coming up the hill. Tiptoe was very sad. Bun tried to comfort her.

'You *must* go to the party,' he said. 'Josie will lend you a frock.' So he went to the little tree house where he usually lived with Josie and Click, and asked Josie for a frock for Tiptoe.

Josie chose a pretty yellow one and hurried up the hill to Jolly Cottage with Click and Bun. She made Tiptoe try on the yellow frock, but it didn't fit her at all.

'I look dreadful in it,' said Tiptoe, peeping at herself in the mirror. 'It's kind of you, Josie, but it's no use. I just can't go to the party. Oh, how I wish that Jolly would come home! I do miss him so. It's nice having dear Bun here, but he's not the same as Jolly.'

Everyone was sad. Josie said she must go home with Click and Bun because it really was nearly time to get ready for the birthday party.

So they opened the door to go down the hill.

And then Josie gave such a squeal that everyone jumped!

'Look! Isn't that Jolly?' she cried. 'But whatever has he got on his head?'

Everybody looked. Sure enough, it *was* dear old Jolly—and on his head he carried the box in which was the new frock he had bought for Tiptoe. He grinned widely and waved to everybody.

'Hello, hello!' he said. 'I've got a fine frock for Tiptoe. And I've sailed a ship to Roll-About Town with an elephant, and nearly got drowned. My word, what adventures I've had!'

Well, Tiptoe squeezed him so hard round the neck that he couldn't breathe, and all the others shook hands and asked him a hundred questions. It was most exciting. Then Josie, Click and Bun said goodbye and ran down the hill to get ready for the party. Then Jolly undid the box and pulled out the frilly frock to show to Tiptoe. How she squealed for joy to see it!

'Oh! I must try it on at once!' she cried. 'Isn't it too beautiful for anything! And oh, look, Jolly! It's got slits at the back so that my wings can go through. I can have wings again! They've been squashed behind my red overall for so long, quite hidden—and now I can show them again. Won't everybody be surprised?'

Tiptoe took off her old red overall. Jolly shook out the frilly frock with its pretty blue bobbles and slipped it over her golden head. Tiptoe put her arms into the short sleeves and there she was, as pretty as a picture! Her wings slid out through the slits at the back of the frock and shone like silver.

'Tiptoe, you're as lovely as a fairy!' cried Jolly. 'And look—put on the shoes. I got those for you too.'

'Oh, Jolly, you *are* kind!' cried Tiptoe joyfully, and she put her tiny pink feet into the blue slippers. Then she danced round the room in glee.

'I shall be just as pretty as anyone at the party!' she said. 'Oh, Jolly, I've missed you so. And I thank you a hundred times for my beautiful frock. Now you wash your hands and brush your hair, and we'll go. It's almost time.'

Jolly didn't know what to do, because the water had made his cap shrink and go small, so it didn't fit him. Tiptoe ran into the soldiers' house next door and borrowed one of their caps for Jolly. He looked quite fine in it.

'I will make you a new one tomorrow,' promised Tiptoe. 'I haven't time now. But you look fine anyway.'

They set off to the party. Mr To-and-Fro lived right down in the town. He had a round house that had a window all the way round it and four little chimneys in the middle. It was a very funny house.

The other guests were arriving just as the two dolls came up. Bruiny the bear wore a pink ribbon and a brooch with B on it.

When the Skittle family came, there wasn't much room to move, because there were so many of them. 'We don't mind if anyone knocks us over,' they said politely to Mr To-and-Fro. 'We are used to that, you know.'

That made everybody laugh, even the pink cat, who kept looking round and about to see if there was any cream for tea. Everyone thought that Tiptoe's wings and new frock were simply lovely, and they told Jolly that he looked very fine in his soldier's cap.

And do you know, when they all pulled crackers after tea, what did Jolly get for his paper hat but a blue sailor's cap. Wasn't that funny! Of course he had to wear it, and looked very grand indeed.

*They set off to the party.*

It really was a lovely party. Mr To-and-Fro had bought heaps of cream buns, the kind that ooze out cream when you bite them. None of the skittles liked cream, so they let the pink cat lick all theirs whenever it squished out of the buns. The cat had a wonderful time and when it had finished, it sat and washed itself for ten minutes.

'Do you want a sponge and towel?' asked Mr To-and-Fro, wobbling over to the pink cat.

'No, thank you,' said the pink cat, 'my left paw is my sponge and my right one is my towel.'

'And which paw is the soap?' asked Bruiny. That made everybody laugh.

You should have seen the lovely presents that everyone brought for Mr To-and-Fro. He had a new blue cup to drink his tea from. He had a large bar of chocolate with nuts in it. He had a game of snakes and ladders and everyone played it because it was such fun sliding down the snakes and going up the ladders—whoooosh—with such a rush!

Then the skittles stood themselves up in a row and invited everyone to throw a wooden ball at them to see if they could knock them down. They had brought the ball themselves which everyone thought was very kind.

Jolly was the best one at knocking them down. With three balls he knocked seven skittles down, and Mr To-and-Fro thought he was so clever that he asked him to try and knock *him* over too.

But Jolly couldn't, because nobody could ever knock Mr To-and-Fro over. He only just wobbled when he was hit and swung from side to side.

'Is it true that you sleep standing up, Mr To-and Fro?' asked Tiptoe shyly.

'Quite true,' said the wobbly man. 'Look— there is my bed. I have stood it straight up against the wall, as you can see. I have to stand upright against the bed and pin the blankets round me to keep them there if I am cold, or else they fall down.'

When it was time to go home they all said goodbye and thank you, and left the little round house. Mr To-and-Fro wobbled to the front door and waved to everyone.

'A lovely birthday party!' cried all the guests as they went home. 'Really lovely.'

But the pink cat had eaten too much cream and felt ill all night, which was rather a pity.

Tiptoe and Jolly went back to their dear little cottage. 'It *is* lovely to be home again,' said Jolly. 'I must take back the soldier's cap. Put the kettle on to make some cocoa, dear Tiptoe, and I will tell you all about my adventures in the *Saucy Sue!*'

And you should just have seen the fairy doll and the sailor doll sitting before the kitchen fire, talking to one another till the clock struck twelve!

# How Bruiny Came to Live Next Door

One day Jolly went down to the town to get a pot of blackcurrant jam for Tiptoe, and he found everyone really most excited.

'The toy fort is finished at last!' cried Mr To-and-Fro, the wobbly man. 'Look—isn't it grand?'

Jolly looked. On the top of the hill on the other side of the town was a fine toy fort. It was made of wood, and was painted red and white. It had four towers, one at each end, and a drawbridge that could be let up and down by chains, for soldiers to march over when they wanted to go in or out of the fort.

'That's for all the toy soldiers in Toyland!' said the pink cat. 'You know, they've had to live in ordinary houses up to now, because there wasn't a proper fort for them to live in. But now one has been built and there it is! Soon all the soldiers everywhere will march up the hill into the fort!'

'It's a marvellous fort,' said Jolly. 'Dear me—
I wonder if the wooden soldiers who live next
to us will have to go too. How we shall miss
them! They are so smart and polite and kind.'

Jolly ran home to tell Tiptoe. He was just in
time to see the soldiers who lived next door
marching out in line, their captain at their head.

'We're off to live at the fort!' said the
Captain proudly. 'The lead soldiers are going
to live there too. So all the soldiers will live
together now, in a proper fort, and we shall be
able to guard Toyland well.'

'Tiptoe! Come and say goodbye to the
soldiers!' cried Jolly. 'They're going!'

Tiptoe ran out. She shook hands with all the
soldiers. Then she and Jolly thought it would be
fun to go with them and see them march over
the drawbridge into the fort. So they ran beside
them, down the hill, through the streets of the
town and up the hill beyond. The drawbridge
was let down, of course, and hundreds of toy
soldiers of all kinds were marching over it into
the grand toy fort.

A band stood nearby playing them into the
fort. 'Tan-tan-tara!' went the trumpets. 'Rub-a-
dub-dub, dub-dub, dub-dub!' went the drums.
It was all most exciting.

*Marching into the fort*

When the soldiers were safely in the fort, the drawbridge was pulled up. Now nobody could get in or out. The soldiers stood in their places, saluted and then marched about when their captains shouted orders.

'We *shall* miss the soldiers next door!' sighed Tiptoe. 'They were so nice, and I did feel so safe with such a lot of brave men nearby. Let's go and call on Josie, Click and Bun, Jolly.'

The two of them set off to the little tree-house—but on the way they met Bruiny, the little brown teddy bear, and he was crying bitterly. He had a big red handkerchief up to his eyes, and he didn't see Tiptoe and Jolly. He walked straight into them, bump!

'Bruiny! Whatever's the matter?' cried Tiptoe, in alarm. 'Have you hurt yourself?'

'No, but something has hurt my house,' said Bruiny. 'Come and see.'

He took them to where his little brick house had been and there it was, all knocked down.

'I am sure one of those great big clumsy rocking horses has been along this way,' sobbed Bruiny. 'And he must have rocked himself over my dear little house. That's the worst of those rocking horses—they're so big that they just don't look where they're going!'

'Come and get some more bricks to build a new house,' said Tiptoe, taking his hand.

'No. I'm not going to have bricks this time,' said Bruiny, wiping his eyes. 'I've heard that you can build houses of cards. Did you know that? So I'm going to build myself a house of snap cards. I can get some in the town, I know. Come along and help me.'

Well, it wasn't long before the three of them had a pack of snap cards. They were rather big and heavy to carry, so Tiptoe and Jolly took some too. They chose a nice open spot in a field where toy sheep were eating the grass, and began to build a house of cards. You know how to build one, don't you? Well, that's just how the three of them built Bruiny's!

First they leaned two cards against one another and then they put two cards against the sides. Then two cards against the edges of those and then two more cards flat on top. That was the first room. Then they built the next room on top of that, just the same. It was most exciting.

When there were four rooms and the house of cards was quite high, Bruiny said the house was big enough.

'One room shall be the kitchen—the bottom

77

one,' he said. 'The next shall be my sitting room. The next shall be my bedroom and the topmost of all shall be my spare room. Isn't it a lovely house?'

Well, Tiptoe and Jolly thought it didn't look a very comfortable kind of house, but they didn't like to say so. Bruiny asked them to go into the kitchen. So they squashed in between the cards—and alas, Bruiny pushed too hard. Down fell the whole of the house of cards, swish-swish-swish!

So it all had to be built up again. It didn't take long, of course. This time Jolly said they wouldn't go inside because it really was time for them to go home to dinner.

'Well, thank you for helping me,' said the little bear, smiling. 'It's a nice house, isn't it? I shall go and buy myself some furniture for it now. So goodbye. Isn't it funny—there isn't a front door to lock!'

Bruiny went off to the town, and Tiptoe and Jolly went home. They sat down and had a good dinner, for they were hungry.

They had a lot to talk about. First they talked about the soldiers all going to live at the fort and how sad they were not to have them next door any more. Then they talked about poor Bruiny and how his house had got knocked down, and how they hoped that his house of cards would be all right.

'It's got no stairs. How do you think he'll go up to bed?' asked Jolly.

'We didn't put a chimney,' said Tiptoe. 'Where will the smoke go if he lights a fire?'

'Bruiny is rather a silly little bear, though he is a darling,' said Tiptoe. 'He wants somebody to look after him, *I* think.'

All that day Tiptoe and Jolly were busy, taking down their old curtains and putting up clean ones, and taking out their little mats to beat the dust from them. They forgot about the soldiers and the house of cards. But as they were sitting down to supper, they heard the sound of soft footsteps. Then they heard the sound of somebody crying and a knock on the door. Jolly opened it.

Outside stood Bruiny the bear, crying into his red handkerchief again. 'Can I come in?' he asked. 'I've nowhere to sleep tonight and I'm very, very unhappy.'

'Oh, Bruiny dear! Of course you can come in!' cried Tiptoe. 'Come and share our supper. What has happened to your dear little house?'

'A lot of things happened to it,' said poor

Bruiny, wiping his eyes, and looking more cheerful when he saw a nice supper on the table. 'First of all, Mr To-and-Fro came to call, and he wobbled against the walls and knocked the whole house down. So I had to build it up again.'

'Poor Bruiny!' said Jolly, pouring the bear out some cocoa. 'Go on.'

'Well, then I tried to get a wardrobe up into the bedroom, but we forgot the stairs, you know, so I had to throw it up, and it knocked the house down again,' went on Bruiny.

Tiptoe felt as if she wanted to laugh, but she didn't like to.

'Then the rain came and made the cards go soft and wet,' said Bruiny, 'and I had to throw them away and build the house from other cards in the pack. I can tell you I felt pretty tired!'

'Poor Bruiny!' said Tiptoe again. 'Eat your sausage roll. You'll feel better then.'

'Well, I got a new house of cards built again and went into the kitchen to have a rest,' said Bruiny, 'and I fell fast asleep. Suddenly I woke up in a dreadful fright! The house was falling about my ears! Swish-swish—it all fell down. And do you know why? It was because the silly toy sheep in the field had bumped against it in the dark!'

'Never mind, Bruiny,' said Jolly, a great idea coming into his head. 'I've got a fine plan! The house next door is empty, because the wooden soldiers have all gone to live in the fort. What about *you* living there, next to us? Then Tiptoe can look after you a bit and we can all have fun together!'

Well, Bruiny was so happy that he swallowed a whole sausage roll at once, and choked. It really was a marvellous idea.

And the next day Bruiny moved into the soldiers' old cottage, and hung up pretty curtains of blue. Tiptoe and Jolly helped him, and the clockwork clown came over too, very pleased that old Bruiny was going to live so near.

'Well, this *is* a bit of luck!' said Bruiny, when the house was finished and a kettle was singing on his toy stove. 'A nice little house and nice little friends next door! I *am* glad my old house was knocked down flat!'

And that is how Bruiny came to live next door to Tiptoe and Jolly. Won't they all have fun together?

# A Grand Visitor

Now once there was great excitement in Toyland because a grand visitor was expected. He was to stay at the toy castle up on the hill.

'He comes once a year,' said Bruiny to Tiptoe. 'Guess who it is!'

But Tiptoe couldn't. 'Well, I'll tell you,' said Bruiny, feeling most important because he knew something that Tiptoe and Jolly didn't know. 'It's Father Christmas!'

'*Really*!' cried Tiptoe, surprised. 'What does he come here for?'

'Can't you guess, silly?' cried Bruiny. 'He comes to get toys from Toyland to put into his sack, to take to children.'

Tiptoe and Jolly looked rather frightened. They had once belonged to children. They had been in a nursery where the other toys had been unkind to them, so they had run away together to Toyland. Now the very idea of going back to a nursery filled them with alarm.

What—leave dear little Jolly Cottage and go right away? And suppose Tiptoe was taken to one house and Jolly to another? Suppose they never saw one another again?

But all the other toys thought it was a great adventure to go into Father Christmas's sack and be taken to the world of children. They talked about nothing else all day long. How they hoped they would be chosen!

Toy Town itself began to be very crowded and busy as the day drew near for Father Christmas to come. All the balls from Roll-About Town came along, rolling and bouncing in glee, wondering if they would be put into somebody's stocking.

The big rocking horses came too, rocking themselves down the streets. Nobody liked them very much, because they were so big and didn't always look where they were going.

The humming tops came with their beautiful hums. They spun down the streets and looked out for Father Christmas. Toy motor cars whizzed along; toy rabbits, cats and dogs ran about with new ribbons round their necks. It really was most exciting.

Everyone was happy and excited except poor Jolly and Tiptoe. They simply couldn't bear to think that they might be taken away from dear old Toyland and all their friends. They shut themselves up in their cottage and wondered if they dared to stay there all the time that Father Christmas was visiting Toyland.

'If we stay in our cottage he won't see us and then he can't choose us to go into his sack,' said Jolly.

So they stayed inside Jolly Cottage and didn't go out at all, except when they had to fetch food from the market. And one morning, as they were buying carrots and onions, there was a great commotion.

'Father Christmas is coming! He's coming!' shouted Mr To-and-Fro, wobbling so much that he almost knocked Tiptoe over. 'Hark! Can you hear his sleigh-bells?'

Tiptoe and Jolly couldn't get out of the crowd. They stood trembling there, hoping that Father Christmas wouldn't see them. Then along came a fine sleigh drawn by four reindeer, tossing their fine antlers in the air. And there was jolly old Father Christmas sitting in the sleigh, holding the reins in one hand and waving to everyone with the other. At his side was an enormous sack, quite empty.

'*Father Christmas is coming!*'

'See his sack? That will be full of toys when he leaves tonight!' whispered Mr To-and-Fro. 'I wonder if you or Jolly will be in it, Tiptoe.'

Tiptoe turned pale. 'Please let's go home, Jolly,' she said.

Father Christmas went by. He caught sight of the sailor doll and the little fairy doll, and waved to them. Jolly waved back, but Tiptoe didn't. She really felt quite ill.

As soon as Jolly could get out of the crowd, he took Tiptoe's arm and hurried her away. They went up the hill and into their little cottage. Jolly shut the door and locked it. He shut the windows, too.

'I like Father Christmas very much,' he said to Tiptoe. 'But I couldn't just bear him to take either of us away, Tiptoe. Now, don't cry. We are safe here.'

The two dolls stayed at home all day. They did not know what was going on at all. They heard shouts and cheers, but they did not even go to the window to look down the hill.

Father Christmas was giving a grand party. Everyone was there, down to the smallest ball. Josie, Click and Bun were there, and they looked about for Tiptoe and Jolly, and wondered where they could be.

At the end of the party came the grand Choosing Time. Every toy had to march past Father Christmas and he said whether or not he would have them for his sack.

Only balls that bounced well, only tops that hummed properly, toy animals that were quite perfect, and dolls that looked happy and smiley were chosen.

Father Christmas was up in the big toy castle, sitting on his throne, his red cloak flowing out round him. He sat there, big and jolly, making jokes as the toys marched by.

'You, little red ball, come along into my sack! You'll go into the foot of a stocking very nicely!'

And the little red ball, with a bounce of excitement, rolled into the enormous sack that Father Christmas was holding open.

'And you, baby doll, come along in!' cried Father Christmas. 'I know a little girl called Ann who will love to have you. And you, humming top, spin into my sack! I've a boy on my list called Michael, he'll love to spin you and hear you hum! And you, blue cat, come into my sack. I'll take you to a small girl called Shirley.'

So the toys marched or rolled or spun into

the big sack. And when all of them had passed by, Father Christmas looked a bit puzzled.

'That's strange,' he said. 'I thought I saw a pretty fairy doll and a jolly sailor doll this morning. I would have liked to take them with me. Are they here?'

'No, they're not,' said Mr To-and-Fro, looking all round. 'But I know where they live. I will get them.' So he wobbled off as fast as he could and was soon knocking on the door of Jolly Cottage. When he told the two dolls what he had come for, they looked very frightened and miserable.

But they had to go with Mr To-and-Fro. Soon they were standing in front of Father Christmas, and he smiled at them.

'Cheer up, dolls! I've some good news for you! I'm going to take you with me! March into my sack—and then I must go!'

So poor Tiptoe and Jolly had to march into the big open sack, which was now almost full to the top with toys of all kinds. Father Christmas closed the neck of the sack and swung it over his shoulder.

'Goodbye, Toys!' he said cheerfully. 'See you again next year. Happy Christmas!'

And off he went to his reindeer sleigh, his

sack over his shoulder. He got in, took the reins and clicked to his reindeer. 'Jingle-jingle,' the bells rang as the reindeer set out for the gates of Toyland.

'We're leaving dear Toyland behind,' whispered Jolly, his eyes full of tears.

'We shan't see our dear little cottage any more,' wept Tiptoe.

'We didn't say goodbye to Bruiny or the clockwork clown,' sobbed Jolly. 'Oh, I'm so unhappy. I know you will go to one home and I shall go to another. We shall never, never see one another again. Oh, Tiptoe, I'm so miserable!'

Now the two toys were near the top of the sack, which was still over Father Christmas's shoulder. Their tears trickled out and fell down his neck. He felt them, wet and warm, and was most astonished.

'Where's this water coming from? he wondered. 'It's not raining!' He stopped his reindeer and opened the sack. Out fell Tiptoe and Jolly, still weeping bitterly. Father Christmas stared in surprise.

'What's the matter?' he asked at last. 'Aren't you pleased to be going with me?'

'Oh, Father Christmas, we've both been in a

nursery before,' said Jolly, wiping his eyes and trying to be brave, in case Father Christmas was cross with him. 'And we weren't happy, so we ran away to Toyland, and we've got such a dear little cottage and we were so happy.'

'And now we have got to say goodbye to one another, and we just can't bear it!' sobbed poor Tiptoe.

'Dear me! Why didn't you tell me you had been out in the big world before and had lived in a nursery?' asked Father Christmas. 'Don't you know that toys are only allowed to go out into the world once? There aren't enough adventures to go round more than once, you know. You are taking somebody else's turn!'

'Oh, we didn't know, we didn't know!' cried Jolly. 'May we go home again then? Oh, may we?'

'You'll have to,' said Father Christmas, smiling kindly at them. 'Off you go. We're at the gates of Toyland, so you'll have to walk a good way home. But I don't expect you'll mind that!'

'Goodbye!' said Jolly and Tiptoe, scrambling out of the big sleigh. 'Goodbye—and thank you very much!'

'Jingle-jingle'—the reindeer sped out of the gates of Toyland, and left Jolly and Tiptoe standing there by themselves. They flung their arms round one another in joy. 'We're still together after all!' said Jolly, wiping away Tiptoe's tears. 'Cheer up. We'll soon be back at Jolly Cottage. And won't everyone be glad to see us!'

So back they went—and oh, how sweet their little house looked, as they came up the hill! How glad everyone was to see them back!

'It's lovely to be home again,' said Jolly, as he unlocked the door. 'Now, Tiptoe, we'll live happily here for ever after. You just see if we don't!'

And I expect they will, don't you?

# We Don't Want to Go to Bed

Polly and Peter didn't like bed-time. It was always far too soon for them. Polly was eight and Peter was seven, and they went to bed at half-past six, which was just about right for that age.

But when half-past six came and Mother said 'Bed-time! Put your toys away!' what a howl there was from Polly and Peter.

'Oh Mother—just ten minutes more!'

'Oh Mother—can't we have just one more game?'

It was always the same and Mother got rather tired of it. 'When you are older you can go to bed later,' she said. 'But seven and eight-year-olds need a great deal of sleep. You will always find that those children who go to bed later than they should are too tired in the morning to do their lessons well, so they are never top of their class.'

Polly and Peter were both top of their

classes, and Mother was glad about that. 'You wouldn't be if you went to bed late!' she often told them and she was right.

All the same, Peter and Polly were naughty at bed-time, and always made a fuss, night after night.

'I want to stay up late,' said Polly, sulking.

'I want to go to bed ever so late,' said Peter. 'Why can't we? It won't do us any harm just for once, Mother. Why can't we?'

'Very well,' said Mother, quite unexpectedly one night. 'I'm tired of this fuss. Stay up as late as you please! Just see how you like it.'

Well, Peter and Polly were so pleased and excited. The clock struck half-past six and they didn't have to put away their toys. It struck seven and still they were up! Daddy came home and was astonished to see them both up.

Mother and Daddy had their supper as usual; Peter and Polly had theirs by themselves. It was some rice pudding. Usually they ate their supper in bed. It was exciting to eat it by the fire downstairs.

After they had had their supper they looked at one another. 'What shall we play?' said Polly.

'Snap!' said Peter. So they got out the snap cards. After that they played snakes and ladders. Then the clock struck eight. Suddenly Polly yawned. She shut her mouth quickly and looked at Peter.

'I didn't yawn because I felt tired,' she said. 'My mouth sort of ached a bit and I had to open it.'

'I feel like that too,' said Peter, and he yawned a very big yawn. 'What shall we play now?'

They got out their bricks and began to build a big castle. But when Polly knocked part of it down by accident, Peter was cross and scolded her.

'You're getting tired and cross,' said Polly. 'You're too little to stay up late.'

'I am not,' said Peter, crossly. 'I won't have you saying things like that. I'm not tired and I'm not cross.'

'Well—you sound cross,' said Polly. 'Let's play something else.'

The clock struck nine and Big Ben, on the wireless, boomed out too. Once or twice the children had heard him when they happened to be awake in bed. It was fun to hear him downstairs. They felt very grown-up, listening to the nine o'clock news.

At ten o'clock, when the children were

playing snap once more—though they didn't see the snaps as often as they should—Mummy and Daddy got up to go to bed.

'I feel tired,' said Daddy. 'I've had a hard day at the office. Let's go to bed.'

'Well, goodnight, children,' said Mother. 'Put yourselves to bed when you feel like it and don't make too much noise, because Daddy and I will be asleep.'

The children were left alone by the dying fire. It was strange to think they were the only ones up. Jane the maid had gone to bed too.

Polly yawned widely again. She could hardly keep her eyes open, but she wasn't going to say so. Peter looked very tired, but he smiled bravely and said, 'Let's play ludo.'

They got out the ludo board and began to throw the dice. Then suddenly they heard a noise.

'What's that?' said Polly, in alarm. It was a strange gurgling noise. She didn't like it at all. She sat very close to Peter. The two children were frightened. The noise went on and on. At last Peter bravely went to the door and looked into the dark passage.

'It's only the water filling up the cistern!' he said at last. 'Mother's had a bath. I suppose the noise sounds louder than usual because the house is so quiet.'

They sat down again. It was getting rather cold, because the fire was almost out. Mother had said they mustn't touch it, in case they got burnt.

Both children would have liked to go to bed—but they didn't like to say so. They were hungry now too, for it was a long time since they had had anything to eat. They went on with their game, but they didn't enjoy it very much.

Then they heard a scratching noise. What could it be? It was at the garden door. Polly didn't like it. It was something that wanted to get in. She clutched at Peter.

'Peter, the house seems different late at night. I'm frightened. What's that scratching noise?'

Peter was frightened too. 'Well,' he said, 'I think perhaps it must be the cat. You go and see, Polly.'

But Polly wouldn't and Peter wouldn't, either. Then they heard a mew and they knew for certain it was Fluffy the cat. They were glad.

Polly went to open the door and let her in. Fluffy leapt in gladly and rubbed against Polly's leg. The little girl took her into the room

*Left alone by the dying fire*

and let her cuddle on her lap. The children were glad to have Fluffy there with them.

Eleven o'clock struck. Peter was so tired that his head kept dropping on to his chest. Polly shook him.

'Peter! Keep awake! We don't want to go to bed yet. Let's keep up till midnight. Think what fun it will be to tell the other children!'

Peter thought the best fun in the world at that moment would be to creep into his warm bed, but he didn't say so. He sat up again.

Then suddenly there came the sound of a loud rapping at the garden door and a deep voice called out, 'Anyone about?'

Polly squealed in fright. Peter went pale. Who could this be, rapping on the door in the middle of the dark night, asking if anyone was about? Policemen? Burglars? Peter was very frightened.

The rapping came again. 'Anyone up?' called the voice. 'What's this door open for?'

Polly gave another scream and tore upstairs to her mother's room. She flung herself on to the bed and clutched her mother.

'Mother! Mother! Come quick! There's a robber or something downstairs!'

Daddy went down and found that a big

policeman had noticed the garden door standing open, and had come to warn the house about it. He had seen the light shining between the cracks in the curtain and had known someone was up.

Polly had left the garden door open when she had let Fluffy in! Oh dear, how she sobbed and cried and wailed, because she had been frightened and was so tired and cold and hungry. Peter cried too.

Soon they were both in bed, their eyes shutting even as their heads touched the pillow. And, oh, how hard it was to wake up in the morning! But Mother made them get up at the usual time and go to school.

They were almost too tired to eat their breakfast. They couldn't remember their tables at school and were sent to the bottom of the class. They yawned so much that Miss Brown got cross.

'If I didn't know that you had a very sensible and good mother, who sends you to bed at the right time, I should think you had one who let you stay up late!' she scolded them.

Polly and Peter didn't like to say they stayed up till midnight. It seemed rather silly now and, oh, how tired they were! It really was too much bother to do any lessons. Polly could quite easily see that if she went to bed late each night she would be at the bottom of the class, like Joan Long, who always went to bed late, instead of at the top as she usually was.

That night the children kept looking at the clock. When would half-past six come? They wanted to go to bed. They were tired and sleepy and cross. Half-past six would never come!

But it did—and just as it struck, Polly spoke: 'Half-past six! Bed-time! Oh, good! Let's put our things away quickly, Peter.'

Mother didn't say anything. She just smiled away to herself. I know why she smiled, don't you? She knew she wouldn't have any more bother with Peter and Polly at bed-time. And she never did.

# Mr Put-Em-Right

There was once a boy whose name was Robert, but he was always called Bossy. It was a very good name for him too, because he was always trying to boss the other children and put them right, and tell them to do things this way and not that way.

Bossy was a big boy for his age, bigger than the others. It wasn't easy to stand up to him and nobody dared to call him Bossy to his face. So they had to put up with him—but how he did spoil their games!

'We won't play this game, we'll play another game!' he would say, as soon as he came up. 'I'll be the chief one. Harry, you can go over there. Jack, you go over there. Now, you listen to me and I'll tell you exactly what to do.'

Bossy liked to tell the others what to spend their money on too, when they had any. 'No, don't get peppermints,' he would say. 'Get toffee today. It's nicer.'

'But I want peppermints,' Jack would say.

'Well, you just buy toffee today, and you'll see I'm right,' Bossy would tell him. And he would march poor Jack off to the sweet shop and see that he bought toffee. Bossy liked toffee very much—much better than peppermints.

Another thing that the children didn't like about Bossy was the way he found fault with them. 'Your dress is torn,' he would say to Jane. 'You'd better go home and get it mended.' Or he would tell Katy to stop singing. 'I don't like your voice,' he would say, putting his hands over his ears. 'Do stop. You are out of tune.'

So, altogether, Bossy was not very much liked. But because he was so big and so loud-voiced and so determined to have his own way, the other children found it very difficult to go against him.

Now, one day Mr Put-Em-Right's garden boy fell ill. Mr Put-Em-Right lived in a small cottage at the end of the village and nobody knew very much about him. They knew he was a sharp-eyed little man, who kept his cottage and garden beautifully, and paid his bills every week, but they didn't know anything else about him.

Well, when his garden boy fell ill, Mr Put-Em-Right pinned a notice on his gate.

'Wanted. Garden boy for one week. Good wages.'

It was holiday time. The bigger boys looked at the notice and thought it would be a good chance to get a little extra money. Bossy saw the notice too.

'I shall apply for that job,' he said to the others. 'I could do with some extra money. I want a new bell for my bicycle and a new pump too. I've heard that Mr Put-Em-Right pays very well.'

'I thought I'd apply for the job, too,' said Jack, and Harry said the same.

'You're smaller than I am,' said Bossy, and he threw out his chest and stood on tiptoe. 'See how big I am. I'm strong, too. I bet I could do the garden work easily—far better than you could.'

'Well, I'm going to go after the job now,' said Jack, but Bossy pushed him back. 'No, you're not. I'm going first.' And off he went to Mr Put-Em-Right's cottage.

Well, Bossy certainly seemed a big, strong sort of lad, so Mr Put-Em-Right told him he could start the next morning and he would be paid every day. The work was not hard. The hours were not long. Bossy went home in delight—all

103

that money for work he often had to do for nothing in his father's garden! Marvellous!

He went off the next morning on his bicycle. He met Jack and Harry, and they scowled at him. As usual, Bossy had got in first and got what he wanted! Bossy waved to them and shouted cheerfully.

He put his bicycle by the back door. Mr Put-Em-Right came out and looked at him. 'Good morning,' said Bossy.

'Say 'Good morning, Mr Put-Em-Right!' or 'Good morning, *sir*,'' said the old man. 'Good gracious me, your face is dirty. Didn't you wash it this morning? Go and wash under the tap. And smooth your hair down, it's sticking up in a very silly manner.'

Bossy opened his mouth to say that he must have got his face dirty on the way there and the wind had blown his hair untidy, but Mr Put-Em-Right silenced him at once.

'No sauce now, not a word from you, understand?'

Bossy washed his face and did his hair. He went out to find Mr Put-Em-Right looking at his bicycle. 'Look here, my boy,' said the old man, pointing a disgusted finger at the bicycle, 'is that the way to keep a nice bike? Look at the dirty wheels! Now, don't answer me back, but you see that you get a rag this evening as soon as you've finished your work, and clean that bicycle properly before you go home.'

Bossy went red. He wasn't used to being ticked off like this and not being allowed to say a word himself. Mr Put-Em-Right showed him the tool shed. 'Now there are the tools,' he said. 'I want those peas over there in the garden well-sticked today. I want the strawberry bed weeded. I want those lettuces thinned out properly. I want the grass cut. You'll find all the tools here. Now get on with your work.'

Well, Bossy got out the lawn mower first and began to cut the grass. But in a minute or two the old man was out again. 'For goodness' sake, don't go round and round the lawn like that, go straight up and down!'

'I don't see that it matters,' said Bossy in surprise. 'This is the way I always do it at home.'

'You're going to do it my way,' said Mr Put-Em-Right firmly. 'I know best. My way is always best. You do as I tell you.'

It was the same with the peas. Bossy felt that he really couldn't go wrong with the peas. It was easy to stick peas. But no. Out came Mr

Put-Em-Right, pulled up all the sticks he had put in and scolded him for being silly.

'Put *two* rows of sticks, not one,' he said. 'Doesn't a boy like you know anything at all? Here you are, sticking the stakes into the roots of the peas and killing them; put a row on each side of the peas!'

'But,' said Bossy, and that was as far as he got.

'I don't want to hear any buts,' said the old man. 'You think you know everything. You're the silliest boy I've ever come across. Do as you're told! My goodness, look where your big feet are treading—all on those young turnips. Come off at once! Why didn't you wear boots to garden in, instead of those silly shoes? You must wear boots tomorrow.'

'They're not mended,' said Bossy.

'Well, I will pay you tonight if you work a bit better than you have done so far,' said Mr Put-Em-Right. 'You can take your boots to my cousin the cobbler and he will mend them well tonight. Then you can wear them tomorrow.'

'But I don't want to spend my . . .' began Bossy. He didn't finish. Mr Put-Em-Right told him he didn't know what was good for him. He said he knew better than Bossy. He told him

*'Do as you're told!'*

he was only a silly young boy, without an idea in his head. He was altogether most annoying and unpleasant.

'Bossy old fellow!' thought Bossy, driving in the pea sticks with quite a lot of bad temper. 'I can't get a word in!'

Mr Put-Em-Right found fault with the way Bossy did the strawberry bed. He said he hadn't thinned the lettuces properly. 'Did you water them first so that the thinnings would come up easily? Did you pull out the tiny ones instead of the well-grown ones? No—you didn't. You're a foolish boy who doesn't use what few brains he's got! Pull up your stockings, boy. Put your tie straight. Smooth down that hair of yours! Tie up that left shoe! You want taking in hand. Well, I'll see what I can do this week!'

Poor Bossy! What a time he had! Mr Put-Em-Right found fault with him every hour of the day. He bossed him all the time. He made him do things his way and not Bossy's way. He kept telling Bossy that everything he did could be done better. He even told Bossy how to spend his money each evening and what was more, saw that he did it!

So his first day's wages went on having his old boots mended. His second day's money went on buying a birthday present for his mother. He happened to mention to Mr Put-Em-Right that his mother was having a birthday, and the old man at once said that he must certainly spend all of his money on her.

'Well, I thought I would spend half of it,' said Bossy, in alarm. Mr Put-Em-Right wouldn't hear of it. 'Such meanness!' he said. 'A nice mother like that and you can't even spend a few coins on her when you've got them. Now you come with me, and we'll go to my friend the jeweller's and see if he has a really nice brooch.'

And off he went with Bossy that evening and insisted that he bought a pretty brooch with M in the middle for Mother.

Bossy's next wages went on getting three panes of glass mended in the cucumber frame. Bossy had dropped a spade by accident and it had fallen on the frame, cracking three of the panes. Mr Put-Em-Right had flown into a temper about that. 'You'll spend today's money on getting that frame mended!' he yelled. 'You're a careless boy! I wish I had my old garden boy back.'

'Was he so good?' asked poor Bossy, who was now beginning to feel that he wasn't so wonderful after all as he had always thought himself to be.

'He's a better boy than you will ever be, because he doesn't think he knows everything, as you do!' said the old man. 'You think you could run this garden yourself, don't you; you think you know better than I do. You think you're a marvellous chap who ought to get his own way all the time! Well, you're not. You're a silly, bossy little fellow who wants a good lesson. And I'll see you get it this week.'

He did. Bossy couldn't seem to do a thing right. He was bossed here, there and all over the place. Many times he thought of throwing down the tools and walking out—but he was afraid of the sharp-tongued Mr Put-Em-Right, so he didn't. He fell silent and, looking gloomy and cross, he tried to do exactly as he was told.

Mr Put-Em-Right spent his next wages for him, as he had done the others, and would not listen to Bossy when he objected. No, off he marched with him and the money was spent in the way Mr Put-Em-Right suggested, and not in the way that poor Bossy had planned. He could see that he wasn't going to buy the bicycle bell and pump after all!

On the last day the old man paid him his last few coins. 'There you are,' he said. 'Spend it how you like.'

Bossy stared at him in surprise. He had quite expected Mr Put-Em-Right to tell him how to spend it. The old man laughed out loud.

'You think I'm a horrid, bossy, grumbling old man, don't you?' he said. 'Well, I'm not. You ask Alfred, my gardener, if I am or not. I've just been giving you a lesson, that's all!'

'What do you mean?' said Bossy, in amazement.

'Well, I know your nickname is "Bossy",' said Mr Put-Em-Right, with a grin, 'and I've heard you bossing all your friends and putting them right, and telling them to do things *your* way, and not theirs. So when you came after this job I thought I'd show you how it felt to be bossed by somebody older and bigger than you. How did you like it?'

'Not at all,' said Bossy, very red in the face. 'I didn't like you either.'

'Of course you didn't,' said Mr Put-Em-Right. 'Nobody likes bossy people. I hate them myself. Well, you can keep your money and spend it how you like — you deserve to because you stuck at the job so well. There's good stuff in you, Bossy, if you use it the right way. What about trying?'

'Right, sir,' said Bossy, still very red. 'Er— thank you, sir. Good day, sir.'

He went off on his bicycle, thinking very hard. Did the other children hate him as much as he had hated old Mr Put-Em-Right? Had he been as annoying and tiresome as the old man had been to him, always finding fault and wanting things done *his* way, and no other? Did they really call him Bossy behind his back?

Bossy didn't buy his bicycle pump and bell. He went to the sweet shop and bought a big bag of sweets and chocolates! For once he was doing something that the other children would like, instead of doing something *he* wanted to do!

He shouted to his friends: 'Hi! I've finished my week's job. Come and share in what I've bought with today's wages!'

They did. They were pleased. Bossy seemed changed, but they didn't know why. 'It won't last!' said Jack to Harry. 'I bet old Bossy is just showing off because he's earned a bit of money!'

But it did last. It's true he is a leader now— but he isn't bossy. He's very friendly with old Mr Put-Em-Right now, too, and grateful to him for taking the trouble to put *him* right. So there must have been very good stuff in Bossy after all!

# What Wonderful Adventures

When the sailor doll came to the nursery all the toys stared at him, for they had never seen a doll like him before.

He wore a sailor suit, a sailor hat and a very wide smile. 'Hello, mates!' he said. 'Ahoy there!'

'What are you?' said the doll in the pink coat.

'A sailor doll,' said the sailor doll.

'Sailors go to sea,' said the teddy bear, who knew quite a lot. 'Have you been to sea?'

The sailor doll hadn't. He didn't even know what the sea looked like. But that didn't worry him.

'Been to sea?' he said. 'Of course I've been to sea! I've been wrecked three times. My, what wonderful adventures I've had!'

The other toys thought he was marvellous to have been to sea and had so many adventures. The pink pig asked him to tell them about an adventure.

'Well, I set sail one fine day and ran into a storm, and my ship overturned,' said the sailor doll. 'I was drowning like anything . . .'

'Ooooh,' said the pig, shivering with excitement. 'Go on. Don't stop like that. What happened?'

The sailor doll thought hard. 'Oh, I caught a big fish, tied a bit of string round its neck, jumped up on its back and made it take me home!'

'You're wonderful!' said the baby doll, and the doll in the pink coat nodded her head too. The sailor doll was pleased. It was nice to be thought so marvellous. Nobody in the toy shop where he had come from had thought him at all wonderful. They had said he talked too much.

Well, after that he was always ready to tell more and more amazing adventures, and the toys listened to him with wide-open eyes and ears.

'One day when my ship was wrecked I was cast on a lonely island where there was nothing but wild animals,' said the sailor doll. 'What do you think I did? I tamed them and taught them to sit up and beg, and then when we were rescued I took them all home with me and sold them to a circus.'

'Did you sell them as wild animals or tame animals?' asked the doll in the pink coat.

'I've forgotten,' said the sailor doll grandly. 'I wish I had kept one. You'd have liked those animals.'

The baby doll didn't think she would, but she didn't say so. She sighed and wished she too could have adventures like the sailor doll. How marvellous to sail off to sea and keep being wrecked and rescued.

The sailor doll behaved very badly, for he told a great many more untruthful stories, and made himself out to be a brave and fearless sailor. The toys thought such a lot of him that he became a kind of king in the nursery. He was soon ordering everyone about and shouting at them, if they were not quick enough.

Then another doll came to the nursery, a wooden skittle, with a cute little head painted at the top. The sailor stared at him.

'You're a skittle, aren't you?' he said. 'Not a doll, just a skittle. Well, you may like to know that I'm head of this nursery.'

'Why are you?' said the skittle.

'Oh, the sailor doll has travelled so far and had such adventures!' said the doll in the pink coat. 'He's been shipwrecked . . .'

116

'And rode home on a fish . . .' said the bear.

'And he's rescued ever so many people from drowning,' said the baby doll. 'Oh, he's *so* brave!'

'How do you know all this?' said the skittle, looking at the sailor doll.

'Well, the sailor has told us, of course,' said the pink pig. 'He's simply marvellous! We're lucky to have him in our nursery with us.'

'You'd better stand in that corner over there,' said the sailor doll to the skittle, pointing to a very dark corner of the toy cupboard. 'I always tell everyone where they are to live. That can be *your* corner.'

'I'd rather have this one, thank you,' said the skittle, and stood in the place that belonged to the sailor doll himself. He was very angry and tried to push the skittle over.

But the skittle didn't mind that a bit. Every time he was knocked over he got up again and his painted face grinned widely. 'I'm made to be knocked over!' he said. 'I'll stay in this corner if I want to.'

But all the toys stood up for their beloved sailor and the skittle could see he was going to have a bad time if he was rude to him, because it was plain that nobody could be friends with him if so. So he said nothing more, but listened in disgust when he heard the sailor doll telling some of his tall stories.

'I can sail any boat there is! I can even sail a steamer by myself. I've only got to see someone in the water and I jump in and rescue them. You should just see me swim! I'm faster even than a fish!'

The skittle had to hear all this and he felt sure the sailor doll was making it all up. 'What a boaster! What a fibber!' he thought. 'But there's nothing I can do to stop him, because all the others admire him so much.'

The skittle was a good fellow. He liked giving a helping hand when he could. He liked a good talk, without any nonsense. He liked a good game and he didn't mind losing, either, so long as the game had been a good one. The toys would have liked him very much if only the sailor doll hadn't always been saying things against him.

Now one day the toys went out for a walk. It was a fine, windy day, and suddenly the sailor doll's hat blew off. It went bowling down the path towards the pond where the ducks lived.

'Oh! My hat, my fine hat!' shouted the sailor doll. 'Bear, go and fetch it.'

The bear and the baby doll went running after the hat. It bowled on merrily, came to the pond and jumped right in. It floated on the water and the sailor doll gave a howl of dismay.

'The ducks will get it! Bear, wade in!'

The bear didn't like to. The water looked deep. The skittle spoke in his wooden voice.

'Wade in yourself! Go on, you're a sailor doll, aren't you? Wade in yourself—swim for your own hat!'

The baby doll ran round the pond, got a stick, leaned over the water and tried to get the hat in to shore with the stick. But alas, she over-balanced and fell splash into the water!

'Save me, save me!' she cried, struggling hard. 'I shall drown, I shall drown!'

Everyone looked at the sailor doll. He could swim, he was brave, he was quite fearless, he had saved heaps of people from drowning— now he would be brave again and jump in and save the baby doll.

But he didn't. 'Go on,' said the bear. 'Jump in or the baby doll will drown.' He gave him a push.

'Don't!' said the sailor doll, turning pale. 'I—I can't swim!'

'Well, fetch the boat from the toy cupboard

and launch it on the pond, and sail it to the baby doll!' cried the pink pig. 'Quick, quick!'

'I-I-I c-c-can't sail a boat!' stammered the sailor doll. 'Don't make me try. I should fall in and drown. I can't swim or sail a boat.'

'Then jump in and get the doll!' shouted the skittle, in disgust. 'Do *some*thing!'

But the sailor doll turned and ran away. Oh, the little boaster, oh, the little coward!

It was the wooden skittle that came to the rescue. He threw himself into the water and landed near the baby doll. 'Catch hold of me now. I'm floating!' he cried. 'Catch hold of me. I'm wood and I shan't sink. Get astride me and waggle your legs in the water, and we'll get to shore all right.'

So the baby doll caught hold of him, got her legs across him, worked them hard and managed to paddle like that to the bank of the pond, where everyone pulled them in to shore.

'You marvellous skittle!' said the baby doll, and hugged him.

'Wonderful fellow!' said the doll in the pink coat.

'Brave and fearless skittle!' said the pink pig. 'A real hero!'

'Pooh!' said the skittle, drying himself by

*'Save me, save me!'*

rolling on the grass. 'Pooh! That's the kind of thing you said to that cowardly sailor doll.'

'Ah, but he only *said* brave things—you *do* them!' said the bear. 'We shan't think anything of him now. You shall be head of the nursery.'

The poor sailor doll hid away when the toys came in. How ashamed he was! He could hardly look the skittle in the face.

'I'm not going to laugh at you,' said the skittle. 'I'm only going to tell you this . . . You've boasted of fine brave deeds and now that the toys see you can't do even one, they turn up their noses at you. Well, if you want to make them friendly again, just turn to and be decent. Look out for some brave deed to do—and DO IT! Don't hide in a corner and cry.'

'Right!' said the sailor doll, in a humble voice. 'I'll try. I really will.'

So he's looking round for a brave deed to do, but one hasn't come along yet. Do you think he'll do it if he gets the chance? I wonder!

# The Girl Who Was
# Afraid of Dogs

Jenny was down by the seaside and she was
having a lovely time. She bathed each day, she
paddled whenever she wanted to, she dug in
the sand and built big castles, and she sailed her
little boat.

After she had bathed, Mummy made her
play ball to get her warm. Mummy threw the
ball and Jenny had to catch it. If she didn't
catch it she had to run after it and that made
her nice and warm.

There was a little dog who belonged to some
other people on the beach and he loved a game
of ball, too. When he saw Jenny playing ball
with her mother, he came up to join in.

But Jenny didn't like dogs. She was afraid
of them. Once a dog had jumped up at her,
asking her to have a game with him, and she
had thought he meant to bite her. So after that
she had always run away from dogs and she
wouldn't be friends at all.

'Darling, you can't go all through your life being afraid of dogs!' said Mummy. 'That's silly. You must never pat strange dogs unless they wag their tails at you, but there's no need to scream and run away whenever one comes near you.'

'I don't like dogs. They're simply horrid,' said Jenny. 'They've got nasty red tongues they put out at me and horrid barky voices, and I don't like them.'

The little dog on the beach was such a friendly little fellow. How he wished Jenny would play ball with him. He belonged to a mistress who was rather old and never played with him. So every day he ran up to Jenny after her bathe and begged to play ball with her.

Jenny had a most beautiful new ball. It was big and blue, and it bounced very well indeed. She was very proud of it because it was nicer than any ball she had ever had. She even took it to bed with her, so you can guess how much she liked it.

She was very angry with the little dog when he tried to join in the game. Whenever she missed the ball her mother threw to her, it rolled away down the beach and the little dog tore after it, yelping in delight.

Jenny wouldn't go near him. She was afraid of him. She stood still and stamped her bare foot on the sand.

'Naughty dog! Horrid dog! Leave my ball alone! I hate you!'

The little dog fetched the ball and dropped it at her feet, wagging his tail. He was hot and his red tongue hung out of his mouth.

'You're a very rude little dog,' said Jenny. 'Put your tongue in! I don't like you. It's no good wagging your tail at me—I know you'd bite me if I came any nearer.'

The little dog sat down and looked sad. He didn't understand why Jenny spoke to him so unkindly. He was such a friendly little dog, not much more than a puppy, and he did so want to be friends with this little girl. She picked up her ball and took it away.

'I shan't play ball whilst that nasty dog is about,' she told her mother. 'I don't like him.'

But the little dog came nearer, hoping that she would throw the ball again. Jenny glared at him. Then she picked up a handful of stones and threw them at him. Two of them hit him and he yelped with pain.

'Oh Jenny! How cruel and unkind!' said Mummy. 'All he wanted was a game—and you hurt him with stones. Now he is limping because his leg is hurt and see how he has put his tail down. He doesn't understand. He is very unhappy.'

The little dog was very sad and puzzled. No one had thrown a stone at him before. Boys and girls don't throw stones at dogs or cats or birds nowadays, unless they are the sort of children that are really bad at heart. And it isn't many children who are bad at heart.

All that day the little dog limped. Sometimes he licked the cut on his leg that the stone had made. Often he looked across at Jenny. He didn't come near her, because now he was afraid of her.

Jenny couldn't help feeling ashamed of herself. All the same she was glad that the little dog kept away. When she saw that he didn't come near her, she took out her ball again and began to play with it by herself. The little dog didn't even watch.

Jenny threw the blue ball high into the air. It fell and she tried to catch it. She missed it and the ball ran quickly down the beach. It ran into the sea. A big wave had just broken and was going back into the sea—and it took the ball with it.

126

'Oh!' yelled Jenny. 'My ball! My blue ball! The sea has got it!'

'You're not to go in after it!' called her mother. 'The sea is too rough today. Those big waves would knock you over.'

'But I want my ball,' wailed Jenny, watching her beautiful blue ball bobbing farther and farther out to sea. 'Oh, my lovely ball!'

She stood there, weeping streams of tears down her cheeks, for she really was very proud of her ball. Now it was gone for ever. It would be thrown up on some other beach, and some other child would find it and play with it. Jenny sobbed bitterly.

The little dog heard her. He had a soft heart and he could not bear anyone to be sad. He jumped up and ran to the edge of the sea. He was still limping. He looked at the ball and he looked at Jenny. He knew quite well what was the matter, because he liked that ball himself. It was a fine ball for a game!

He didn't remember that Jenny had been unkind to him, shouted at him and thrown stones at him. He only remembered that it was her ball and that she was unhappy because the sea was taking it away.

And into the water he paddled after that

ball! A big wave took him off his feet and rolled him over. But he got himself the right way up again and found that he could swim. So out into the deep water he swam, farther and farther out, his pink tongue hanging from his mouth, his legs working quickly.

'Oh! The little dog is saving my ball for me, Mummy!' cried Jenny. 'Look, do look! Oh, Mummy, isn't he a good, brave little dog! He's getting my ball!'

'That's the same little dog you treated so unkindly,' said Mummy. 'What a forgiving little fellow he is!'

'He's got the ball! It's in his mouth! He's got it!' cried Jenny. And so he had. He turned round again and swam for the store, panting, the ball safely in his mouth. He came into shallow water, paddled through it, ran to Jenny and put the ball down at her feet. Then he shook himself, wagged his tail politely and ran back to his mistress.

'Well!' said Mummy. 'That dog behaves far better than you do, Jenny! You shouted at him and threw stones at him and made him limp, when all he wanted was a game with you. But instead of letting you lose your ball he fetched it for you and gave it to you, and

*Saving the ball*

didn't even stay to be thanked.'

'Oh, Mummy, it was so good of him' said Jenny, her face very red, because she did feel that her mother was right—the little dog had behaved much better to her than she had behaved to him. 'Oh, Mummy, I feel dreadful now. Can you say you are sorry to a dog? Would he understand?'

'I don't expect he wants you to come near him again,' said Mummy. 'I should think he is far more afraid of you now than you ever were of him.'

'I know what I shall do,' said Jenny suddenly. 'I shall give him this blue ball, Mummy. I like it very much, but so does he. And perhaps if I give him this ball for his very own he might forgive me for hurting him and he wouldn't be afraid of little girls any more.'

'Well, it would be a very nice thing to do,' said Mummy, looking pleased. 'I always think that when we have done something wrong, the least we can do is to find out some way to put it right. And that might be just the way, Jenny. But won't you be afraid of going up to him? You know how afraid you are of dogs—very silly of you, really, but still, I can't seem to make you different.'

'I *am* afraid of him, because he's a dog,' said Jenny. 'But, all the same, I'm not going to be a coward now. I'm going to give him my ball.'

So she walked across the beach to where the little dog was lying. He raised his head and looked at her. But he didn't wag his tail. He only kept tail-wags for friends and he was sure this little girl was no friend.

'Little dog,' said Jenny, kneeling down beside him. 'I'm sorry I hurt you. You can have my ball for your own. Here you are.'

The little dog lay and looked at Jenny. He still didn't wag his tail. He was afraid of her. He wouldn't take the ball.

'Take it,' said Jenny. 'It's yours.'

But the little dog didn't move, except to turn his head away. Jenny was upset. She put the ball down beside the dog and left it there. Then she stretched out her hand very nervously—and patted him! It was the first time in her life that she had ever patted a dog! She liked it. She liked the feel of the rough, warm coat. She patted him again.

'Good dog,' she said. 'Good little dog.' Then she ran back to her mother, feeling very glad. The little dog got to his feet and stared after her. What a funny girl! She had patted him and called him good dog and, bones and biscuits, she had left her ball beside him! She had given it to him! She was a friend after all!

Joyfully he picked up the ball and sped after Jenny. He wagged his tail so hard that it was difficult to see it. 'Wuff!' he said. 'Play a game, won't you!'

'He's forgiven you,' said Mummy. 'He wants to play with you!'

The little dog dropped the ball for Jenny to throw for him. She threw it and he sped after it and brought it back. She threw it again. Then Mummy threw it for both of them and they had a race to see who could get it first.

And before the day was out the two of them were very good friends indeed. Jenny was patting him and even tickling him, and the little dog was licking her, and jumping up in delight.

'How silly I was to be afraid of dogs!' thought Jenny, when she went to bed that night. 'Why, I like them very much. I'd even like a puppy for my own!'

# A Tin of Yellow Polish

Everyone would have liked Dame Round-Face very much if only she hadn't been such a borrower. She didn't borrow money—she borrowed things like brooms, lawn mowers, a drop of milk, a pinch of tea. And she hardly ever paid for what she borrowed or gave anything back in return.

The people in Snowdrop Village were generous and kind, and they didn't mind lending anything, but they did get tired of seeing Dame Round-Face popping her head in at their kitchen doors and hearing her say:

'*Have* you got a bit of soap you could lend me? I've run out of mine and the shops are shut, and I simply *must* finish my washing!'

If no one was in when Dame Round-Face called, she would just go in and help herself to what she wanted, and that made people very cross.

'What are we to do about it?' they said to

one another. 'We can't let Dame Round-Face go on behaving like this. It's bad for her and makes us feel very cross.'

But they couldn't do anything about it because Dame Round-Face didn't take any notice of them when they spoke to her about her bad habit.

'Oh, I'll pay it back all right,' she would say, but she hardly ever did.

Now one day she wanted some polish to rub up her kitchen taps and her door handles. She had none in her tin. It was quite empty! What a nuisance!

'Never mind—I'll borrow some from Mother Twinkle,' thought Dame Round-Face, and off she went. But Mother Twinkle was out. Dame Round-Face tried the kitchen door. It opened.

'Good!' thought Dame Round-Face. 'I'll just pop in, get Mother Twinkle's polish, and slip back with it. She won't mind, I'm sure!'

She opened the cupboard door and looked on the shelves, to see where Mother Twinkle kept her polish, and suddenly her eye caught sight of a tall, thin tin, bright yellow in colour. Tied round the neck of the tin was a magic duster! Dame Round-Face knew it was a magic one, because it changed colour as she looked at it, a thing that magic dusters always do.

'My!' thought the old lady. 'Now this *is* a bit of luck! Magic yellow polish and a magic duster to polish with! My word!'

It certainly was a bit of luck. The duster was so full of magic that it was quite well able to work by itself, once the polish was tipped out of the tin on to it. It would whisk off to the nearest tap or door handle and polish away like anything. Dame Round-Face wouldn't need to rub at all—the duster would do it all!

She ran back to her own cottage with the tin and the duster, feeling very pleased. She tipped out some of the yellow polish on to the duster and then shook it out into the air. It flew off by itself at once and settled on to the taps over the sink.

'Look at it polishing them!' said Dame Round-Face in delight. 'My goodness me, those taps of mine will shine like the sun!'

They did. They shone so brightly that they seemed like lanterns in the dark corner over the sink. The duster whisked itself about a little and then flew to the door handles. It began to polish away hard.

'You do the cupboard handles for me too,' said Dame Round-Face, settling herself down in her rocking chair. 'I'm going to have a little sleep.'

The duster polished all the door handles and all the cupboard handles. Then it looked around for something else to polish. It saw two brass candlesticks on the mantelpiece and flew off to polish those, first getting itself a little more of the yellow polish out of the tall yellow tin.

When the candlesticks were done the duster couldn't find any more brass to polish. The doors were shut so it couldn't go into any other room to do some polishing there. It felt sad. It went over to Dame Round-Face, but she was fast asleep and her mouth was wide open. Her face shone red.

The duster bent itself gently forward, made itself a point out of one of its corners and carefully polished Dame Round-Face's front teeth. Soon they were a bright, shining yellow. The duster was pleased.

It started on Dame Round-Face's nose next. It polished it very, very gently so that she might not wake. The duster had never polished anyone's face before and it couldn't help enjoying it.

It polished the old dame's nose till it was as bright yellow as the candlesticks. Then it

*Polishing Dame Round-Face's nose*

polished her big ears. Then her cheeks, chin and forehead. It polished away and was quite sorry when it had finished.

It was tired at last and sank beside the tin on the table. After a while Dame Round-Face woke up. She rubbed her eyes, yawned and looked round the room. How the taps, doorhandles and candlesticks shone and twinkled!

'Marvellous!' said Dame Round-Face, very pleased. 'I'd better take the polish and the duster back. If Mother Twinkle isn't home yet, she will never know I've borrowed it!'

Mother Twinkle wasn't home. Dame Round-Face popped the polish back on the shelf, with the duster. She shut the door and hurried home.

'I shan't tell Mother Twinkle I borrowed the duster and polish,' she thought. 'She might be rather cross, as they are magic ones.'

But Mother Twinkle knew as soon as she opened her cupboard door that someone had borrowed her magic yellow polish and duster! For one thing, the duster was dirty, and for another thing, the tin was half empty!

'Now, there's a mean trick to play on anyone!' said Mother Twinkle, crossly. 'To come in while I am out, borrow my things without asking and put them back without so much as waiting to say thank you! I guess it was old Dame Round-Face! I wish I could punish her. But she is sure to say she didn't borrow anything.'

But Mother Twinkle didn't need to punish Dame Round-Face. She was being dreadfully punished, because of the shining yellow polish on her face and ears! When she went out that afternoon, without looking in her mirror first, she couldn't *think* why people stared at her so hard, and then turned away and laughed!

'She's got a yellow nose!' whispered little Twinkle and Lobbo.

'Her ears are shining gold!' giggled Pitapat.

'Her teeth are yellow when she smiles!' laughed Clicky the pixie.

Dame Round-Face hurried home to look in the mirror, to see what everyone was staring at. There she saw her shining, gleaming yellow face, set with highly polished yellow ears! Oh, how dreadful, how dreadful!

'That tiresome duster must have polished me too!' cried Dame Round-Face. 'Oh my, oh my! Now I must go to Mother Twinkle and ask her to take away this dreadful yellow spell.'

How Mother Twinkle laughed when she saw the shining, round, yellow face appearing round her kitchen door.

'Oh, Mother Twinkle, please take away the yellow spell!' begged Dame Round-Face. 'I simply can't bear it. Everyone is laughing at me.'

'You deserve it,' said Mother Twinkle, beginning to laugh again herself. 'I shan't take the spell away. Keep it on your face to remind you not to borrow! It will wear away gradually as you wash each morning and night.'

'And listen to me—although it will slowly fade, Dame Round-Face, it will become yellow again if you borrow anything!' said Mother Twinkle.

Poor Dame Round-Face! The yellow did slowly go away—but it always comes back again if she forgets and begins to borrow anything.

# The Lost Motor Car

Once upon a time, George had a toy motor car that wound up with a little key. It was a yellow car, just big enough to take a little tin man to drive it and one passenger, who was usually somebody out of the Noah's Ark.

One day George took the car out into the garden to play with. But it wouldn't run on the grass very well, even when it was fully wound up, so he left it there and went to fetch something else.

Whilst he was in the house it began to rain and his mother called to him to stay in the nursery until the sun shone again. So George forgot about the toy car and left it out in the garden all day long.

The rain rained on it. Spiders ran all over it. An earwig thought it would make a nice hiding place and hid under the bonnet. A large fly crept there too.

George didn't remember that he had left it

in the garden. He wanted to play with it in two days' time and he hunted in his toy cupboard for it—but of course it wasn't there. So he didn't bother any more, though he was sad not to have the little car, because it really was very nice indeed and could run at top speed twice round the nursery before it stopped.

The little yellow car lost all its bright paint in the next rainstorm. Red rust began to show here and there. Its key dropped out into the grass. The little tin man at the steering-wheel split in half. One of the wheels came loose—so you can see that the toy car was in a very bad way.

And then one morning two little men with baskets came hurrying by. They were pixies, and not much bigger than your middle finger.

In their baskets were loaves of bread and cakes, for the two men were bakers and sold their goods to the Little Folk.

They suddenly saw the old toy motor car and went up to it in surprise. 'What is it?' said Biscuit.

'It's a car!' said Rusky, his brother. 'An old toy car! Will it go?'

They pushed it—and it ran along on its four rusty wheels, though one wobbled a good bit, because it was so loose.

'It *does* go! said Biscuit. 'I wonder who it belongs to.'

'I suppose it belongs to the little tin man at the wheel,' said Rusky. 'But he has split in half, so he's no use any more. I say, Biscuit—if only *we* could have this car! Think how we could take all our loaves and cakes round in no time. Our baskets are sometimes so heavy to carry and when it rains, they get wet. But if we had a car . . .!'

'Oh, Rusky! Do let's have it!' said Biscuit. 'We'll hurry along and deliver our things today, and then we'll come back and see what we can do with the car. It's just falling to pieces there, so we might as well have it for ourselves!'

Well, after about an hour the two little bakers came back. They pushed the car off to their tiny house under the hazel bush and then they had a good look at it.

'It wants a fine new coat of paint,' said Biscuit.

'It wants that wheel tightened,' said Rusky.

'It's got no key,' said Biscuit. 'How will it go?'

'We'll have to rub the wheels with a bit of Roll-Along Magic,' said Rusky, getting excited.

So they set to work. They took the poor little tin man away from the wheel. They screwed the loose wheel on tightly. And then they bought a tin of bright red paint and gave the whole car a beautiful coat of red.

'I think we'll paint the wheels yellow, not red,' said Biscuit. 'It would look more cheerful.'

So the wheels were painted yellow. Along the sides of the car the two bakers painted their names in yellow letters on the red—'Biscuit and Rusky, Pixie Bakers'. When they had finished, the little toy car looked very smart indeed.

'Now for a bit of magic to rub on the wheels!' cried Rusky. So they got a bit of Roll-Along Magic and rubbed it on each of the four yellow wheels. Then in they got and drove the car off for its first spin.

It went at such speed! They tore round the garden path and back, and all the Little Folk came out in surprise to see them. And next day Biscuit and Rusky piled their bread and their delicious little cakes into the car, and drove off to deliver them to all their customers. It didn't take them nearly as long as usual and they were just as pleased as could be!

They even bought a tiny horn for the car that said 'honk-honk!' whenever a worm or a beetle ran across their path. And it was this horn that

*They tore round the garden path.*

George heard one day when he was playing out in the garden near the hazel bush!

He heard the 'honk-honk!' and looked round to see what could be making the noise. He suddenly saw the little red and yellow car rushing along, with Biscuit and Rusky inside, and he stared in such surprise that at first he couldn't say a word. Then he called out:

'I say! I say! Who are you? Stop a minute, do!'

The car stopped. Biscuit and Rusky grinned up at George. He stared down at the car. It looked like the one he had lost, but this was red with yellow wheels and his had been all yellow.

'That's a dear little car you've got,' he said. 'Where did you get it from?'

'We found it under there,' said Rusky, pointing. 'It belonged to a little tin man, who sat at the wheel, but he had split in half, so we took the car for ourselves and painted it brightly. Isn't it fine?'

'You know, it's *my* car!' said George, remembering the little tin man. 'It really is! I must have left it out in the garden. I'm sure I did!'

Biscuit and Rusky stared up at him in dismay. 'Oh dear! Is it really your car? We do love it so—and you can't think how useful it is to us, because we use it to deliver our bread and cakes now, instead of carrying them over our shoulders in baskets. But, of course, if it's yours, you must have it back.'

They hopped out of the car, looking very sad and sorrowful. George smiled at them.

'Of course I shan't take it from you! I shouldn't have left it out in the garden. You've made it simply beautiful—and your names are on it too. You keep it. I'm very pleased to give it to you and I'll often be looking out for you. Do hoot your horn whenever you pass me, will you? Then I'll know you're there.'

# The Strange Butterfly

There was once a man who collected butter-flies. He used to go out into the country with a net and look for any butterfly he still hadn't got in his collection, and try to catch it in his net.

Then he would pop the butterfly into his poison-pot. It would go to sleep there and never wake up again. Then the butterfly man would take it out, spread its wings out to show them properly and put it into his butterfly box, stuck on a pin.

One day he went out with his net to look for butterflies. He could only see cabbage whites, red admirals and peacocks—butterflies he knew very well and had already got.

'This is not going to be my lucky day,' he said to himself. And then quite suddenly he saw a most beautiful butterfly sitting on a flower. It had blue and silver wings with red spots and quite a big body.

'Never seen one like *that* before!' said the

man to himself, and he crept up behind it very, very softly and very, very slowly. He lifted his net—and then suddenly he brought it down, crash! And the beautiful butterfly was caught.

It began to make a noise. It squeaked in a high voice, it fluttered in fright round the big net, it tried its very hardest to get out.

The butterfly man put his hand into the net to get out his prize. And, to his great surprise, the butterfly bit him on the finger! Bit him very hard, too, so that he cried out in pain, took his hand out of the net and looked at his bleeding finger.

A little girl came up and looked at the man in surprise.

'What's the matter?' she said. 'Have you hurt yourself?'

'This butterfly bit me,' said the man.

'Butterflies don't bite,' said the little girl. 'They have no teeth. All they have is a sort of tongue they can unroll and dip into flowers to get the honey.'

'Now don't try to teach me anything about butterflies!' said the man, crossly. 'I have collected them all my life. And this one certainly bit me.'

The little girl saw that the butterfly in the net

was beginning to flutter again. It called out in a tiny squeak of a voice.

'Let me out! Save me, save me!'

'Good gracious! The butterfly is speaking,' said the little girl. 'I heard it.'

'Don't be silly,' said the man. 'It squeaked, that's all. Some caterpillars and butterflies do squeak.'

'This one talked,' said the little girl. She looked into the net quickly and then she gave a loud cry.

'You've caught a fairy! It's a fairy, not a butterfly!'

'There aren't such things as fairies,' said the man. 'You really are a silly little girl. Caught a fairy indeed! I don't believe in fairies and never did.'

'Well, you'll never be able to see one, then,' said the little girl. 'That's why you can't see that this butterfly isn't a butterfly, but a real, live, beautiful fairy. Let her go, please.'

'Certainly not!' said the man. 'It is going to be put into my poison-pot.'

'What—to be killed?' said the little girl in horror. 'Oh, no, no! You mustn't kill a fairy. It's horrid enough to have to kill butterflies, but it would be wicked to kill a fairy. I'll set her free.'

The man grabbed the fairy from the net, opened his poison-pot, and popped the fairy inside. There was just room for her. He put the lid on and there was the fairy inside the poison-pot, breathing the poisoned air there.

The little girl began to cry, but she couldn't do anything. The man set off again with his butterfly net, without even saying goodbye to her.

'I'd better follow him and see what happens to that poor little fairy!' said the little girl. So she did. And, very soon, the man sat down, leaned his head against the trunk of a tree and fell fast asleep.

'Now's my chance!' thought the little girl, and she crept up to where the man had put the poison-pot. She took it and opened it.

The poor little fairy was fast asleep inside. The little girl was frightened.

'Perhaps she will never wake up again,' she thought. 'Oh dear! I'll put her here in the shade of this big leaf and fan her a little.'

So she did—and to her great delight the tiny fairy stirred at last, stretched her lovely silver and blue wings, and sat up.

'I feel ill,' she said.

'There's a dewdrop above your head—drink it,' said the little girl in a gentle voice. The fairy

*'Now's my chance!'*

sipped from the silver dewdrop and felt better. She flew up to the little girl's lap.

'You saved me from that horrid man, didn't you?' she said. 'You are a dear little girl! I'll give you three wishes! You can wish them whenever you like!'

She flew off on her pretty wings. The little girl looked at the sleeping man. She saw that he had a small gold watch in his waistcoat pocket and she giggled. She gently took out the ticking watch, popped it into the poison-pot and put the lid on.

'What a surprise he'll get when he finds his beautiful butterfly is gone and his watch is in the pot instead!' she thought. 'Oh dear, how I do wish that every boy and girl could hear about this funny adventure of mine!'

Well, that was a wish, wasn't it? And, like all magic wishes, it has come true. I'd like to wish a wish, too—I wish I could have seen the butterfly man's face when he opened the pot to show his friends the strange butterfly and found his gold watch there instead!

# A Present for Granny

'It's Granny's birthday tomorrow,' said Cousin Betty to George.

'Oh dear!' said George. 'So it is. And I had forgotten all about it. I haven't any money in my money box to buy her a present.'

'I've got some,' said Cousin Betty. 'I've been saving up. I shall buy Granny two packets of nice hairpins. She will like those. She won't think much of *you*, George, if you don't give her a present.'

'I did have some money before I came away to the seaside,' said George, 'but I spent it on this big spade and a fishing net. Bother! I wish Mummy had reminded me that it was Granny's birthday.'

'I did,' said Mummy, from her deck chair. 'But I expect you forgot in all the excitement of coming to the seaside.'

George was worried. He liked Granny and he liked remembering people's birthdays. He didn't want Cousin Betty to give Granny a present if he didn't. But he knew she would. She always liked to remember things that other people forgot. She would be pleased to think that she would be the only grandchild to give Granny something.

'Well, I simply must give her a present,' thought George, digging hard in the sand. 'I wonder if there is anything she would like that doesn't cost money?'

He wondered if there were any nice shells on the shore. Perhaps if there were he could bore a tiny hole in each and thread them together to make a necklace. So he looked. But there were no pretty shells at all, only great big ones, half-broken.

Then he found a five-fingered starfish lying on the sand. It was the first time George had ever found a starfish and he thought it must be very rare, and quite valuable. He put it into his pail and carried it proudly to Mummy.

'Look what I've got for Granny,' he said. 'A very rare starfish. That would be a lovely present for her, wouldn't it, Mummy?'

'No,' said Mummy. 'I'm afraid Granny doesn't like starfish, darling. And certainly it wouldn't like being a birthday present.'

'Oh, Mummy, do let me give it to Granny,' begged George. 'I'm sure she would like it. I can't find any nice shells to thread.'

'Isn't he silly?' said Cousin Betty to Mummy. 'Fancy thinking of giving a stupid, ugly starfish for a birthday present. I think Cousin George is a baby. He's a baby for not remembering about Granny's birthday and saving up for it, and he's a baby for thinking she would like a silly starfish for a present.'

George nearly threw the poor starfish at Cousin Betty, he felt so angry with her. But he didn't, because he knew the starfish wouldn't like it. He went very red and ran down the beach with his pail. He emptied the starfish into a pool of water.

Then, in the pool, he saw what he thought were beautiful sea flowers. They were sea anemones, red and green, whose feelers waved about in the water like flower petals. They were really sea animals, not sea flowers, but George didn't know that.

'Oh! I'll pick these and take them to Granny!' he thought, pleased. 'They are really lovely.'

But they seemed to be stuck hard onto the side of the rock and he couldn't get them off.

Also, when he touched them, they drew in their pretty feeler-like petals and looked like ugly lumps of jelly. It was very disappointing.

Betty came along, and how she laughed when she saw George trying his hardest to pick the anemones.

'Don't tell me you are going to pick a bunch of those and take them to poor Granny!' she cried. 'What a little silly you are! They are not proper flowers, Cousin George, they are strange little sea animals, all mouth and tummy, with feelers waving round the edge to catch something to eat!'

George really did feel silly then. He couldn't pick off the lumps of jelly—and anyway, they weren't like pretty flowers any more. He glared at Betty.

'You're a horrid girl. Go away. You're always laughing at me. I don't like you.'

He walked off by himself. Then he saw something scuttling quickly along over the sand. George looked at it and saw that it was a small crab—but what a pretty one!

'I've never seen such a dear little crab!' said George. 'Never! It's green and small and it looks so friendly. I do like it.'

He picked up the crab and it seemed to

157

nestle into his hand, curling up its legs under its body. He took it to his mother.

'Mummy! I shall give this to Granny for her birthday. It's the prettiest crab I ever saw in my life, and it's so friendly and tame. Look! It's curled up in my hand. I'm sure Granny would like it for a pet. She said the other day that she hadn't even a cat to pet now. I shall give her this crab.'

'No, darling,' said Mummy. 'It is a dear little crab, I agree. But I am sure Granny would rather not have it. It would soon die. It wouldn't be kind to keep it as a pet.'

Cousin Betty ran up and peered down at the crab. 'Good gracious! You're surely not thinking of giving *that* to Granny, are you? She would *laugh*!'

'She wouldn't,' said George. 'I know she wouldn't. She never laughs at me. Nobody does, except you.'

'Now, don't quarrel,' said Mummy. 'And don't look so disappointed, George. Go and put the poor little crab back on the sand. Granny really won't mind if you haven't a present for her.'

George ran down to the sand. Betty ran after him. 'Let's play with the crab. Let's

'It's a dear little crab.'

pretend he's a spider and our hands are birds going after him, to eat him.'

'No,' said George. 'That would frighten him. He's such a dear little crab.'

Betty made a grab at the crab. George pushed her away and set the tiny thing on the wet sand. Betty pounced on him, but he scrabbled hard with his legs and began to sink down into the sand and disappear. Soon he was gone.

'You can't get him now,' said George, pleased. 'Didn't he disappear quickly?'

George dug about in the wet sand with his fingers, trying to feel if the crab was anywhere about. But he wasn't. George suddenly felt something round and hard down in the wet sand, and pulled it up with his finger and thumb. It was all sandy. George dipped it into a pool of water and cleaned it—and, goodness gracious me, it was a silver coin!

'A coin!' said George, in surprise and delight. 'Mummy, Mummy, look what I've found, just where the little crab sank down—a coin, a silver coin!'

Mummy was very surprised. She sent George to ask the other children on the beach if they had dropped any money, but they hadn't. Mummy said it might even have been lost the year before and stayed buried in the sand till George found it.

'You are very lucky,' she said. You may keep the coin for yourself as we don't know who lost it. We can always give a coin to anyone if we do hear it has been lost.'

'Oh, Mummy, now I can buy a present for Granny!' said George, beaming all over his face. 'A nice present, too. Oh, I *am* glad I put the little crab back into the sand. He found the coin for me!'

George went off to the shops and what do you think he found in one of them? He found a small brooch in the shape of a tiny green crab! It really was very quaint and pretty. He bought it for his Granny.

'It's a much nicer present than my pack of hairpins,' said Cousin Betty, not at all pleased. 'I wish you hadn't found that coin.'

'You're not a very kind little girl, Betty,' said Mummy. 'You have teased George a lot this morning and he was only trying to find something to please his Granny. I should have thought a lot more of you if you had helped him, or had even offered to let him have one of your packets of hairpins to give Granny.'

Then it was Betty's turn to go red. Mummy

didn't often speak to her little niece like that and Betty felt sad.

Granny loved the little crab brooch, and listened in surprise to George's story of how he found a crab which had shown him the lost coin.

'Well, I must say I like a crab brooch better than a live crab!' said Granny, kissing George. 'Thank you for a lovely present, George. It was nice of you to spend the coin on me.'

She liked Betty's hairpins, too, but both George and Betty knew the little crab brooch was much the nicer present.

'I shan't tease you any more, George,' said Cousin Betty. 'It was mean of me. It serves me right that you should have got such a lovely present for Granny.'

'Oh, don't worry about that,' said George. 'The very next coin I find I'll spend on *you*, Betty! I promise you that.'

He hasn't found any more money yet, but you should just see how he digs down after any crab that sinks into the sand! He says he knows another crab will find him a coin. I hope I hear if it does.

# The Quarrelsome Bears

There were once two bears who lived in a little yellow cottage in Toy Town. Teddy was a brown bear and Bruiny was a blue one. And how they quarrelled! Really, you should have heard them!

'That's my handkerchief you are using!' said Teddy.

'Indeed it's not!' said Bruiny.

'I tell you it *is*,' said Teddy.

'And I tell you it's not!' said Bruiny.

'Don't keep telling me fibs,' said Teddy.

'Well, don't you either,' said Bruiny.

That was the sort of quarrel they had every single day. Silly, wasn't it? Especially as they both had plenty of handkerchiefs.

One afternoon they dressed themselves in their best coats and ties to go to a party. They did look nice. Teddy tied Bruiny's bow and Bruiny tied Teddy's. Then they took their new hats and went to the door.

And it was raining! Not just raining quietly, but coming down angrily and fiercely—pitterpatterpitterpatterpitterpatter, without a single stop.

'Goodness! Look at that!' said Teddy. 'We must take our umbrella.'

They had a big red umbrella between them and it was really a very fine one indeed. Teddy looked for it in the umbrella stand. It wasn't there.

'What have you done with the umbrella, Bruiny?' asked Teddy.

'Nothing at all,' said Bruiny, at once. 'What do you *think* I've done with it? Used it to stir my tea with?'

'Don't be silly,' said Teddy. 'That umbrella was there yesterday. You must have taken it out.'

'I did not,' said Bruiny. 'You must have taken it yourself.'

'I haven't been out for two days,' said Teddy. 'What do you think I'd want with an umbrella indoors?'

'Oh, you might use it to tease the cat with,' said Bruiny unkindly.

'Oh! As if I would tease our dear old cat with an umbrella!' cried Teddy angrily.

'Well, perhaps you used it to poke the fire,' said Bruiny.

'And perhaps *you* used it to scrub the floor!' cried Teddy. 'I can think of silly things too. No, it's no good, Bruiny. You took that umbrella for something and you might just as well try and remember what you did with it, and where you put it. Hurry, now, or we'll be late for the party.'

'I tell you, Teddy, I haven't had the umbrella and I don't know where it is,' said Bruiny. 'It would be a good thing if *you* thought a little while and found out where you had hidden it.'

'I don't hide umbrellas,' said Teddy.

'Well, you once hid the cat in the cupboard and it jumped out at me,' said Bruiny.

'That was just a joke,' said Teddy. 'I shouldn't hide our umbrella in the cupboard, because it wouldn't jump out at you.'

'But you'd like it to, I suppose?' cried Bruiny, getting crosser and crosser.

'Yes, I'd love to see an umbrella jump out at you and I'd like to see it give you a good chase!' shouted Teddy, getting angry too.

'You're a bad teddy bear!' said Bruiny, and he pulled Teddy's bow undone.

'Don't!' cried Teddy. He caught hold of Bruiny's coat and the coat tore in half!

'Oh! Oh! Look at that!' wailed Bruiny. 'I'll jump on your hat for tearing my coat!'

And before Teddy could stop him, Bruiny had thrown his new hat on the floor and jumped on it. It was quite spoilt!

Then they were both very silly. They took each other's ties off. They threw both hats out of the window. They even threw each other's handkerchiefs into the wastepaper basket!

And in the middle of all this there came a knocking at the door! Bruiny went to open it, panting. Outside stood Mrs Field Mouse with all her little family. They were on their way to the party, each mouse under its own tiny umbrella.

'Goodness me! What's all the noise about?' asked Mrs Field Mouse severely. 'I knocked three times before you heard me.'

'Well, Mrs Field Mouse,' said Bruiny, 'Teddy has taken our umbrella and doesn't know where he put it.'

'Oh, you fibber!' cried Teddy. 'It's Bruiny that must have taken it, Mrs Field Mouse. We've only got one and it's raining, and we wanted it to go to the party.'

'Dear me!' said Mrs Field Mouse.

'What have *you* come for?' asked Bruiny.

'Well, I came to give you back your big umbrella,' said Mrs Field Mouse with a laugh. 'I suppose you forgot that you both kindly said

# The Quarrelsome Bears

*Jumping on the hat*

I might have it yesterday to go home with my little family, because it was big enough to shelter them all. I promised to bring it back today. Here it is. I'm sorry you should have quarrelled about it.'

She stood it in the hall stand and then went off to the party with her little family. How they squealed when they heard the joke!

'Well, I never,' said Bruiny, looking at the umbrella. 'So you didn't take it, Teddy.'

'And you didn't either,' said Teddy. 'Oh dear, how silly we are! We've got our umbrella, but we've spoilt our suits and bow ties, and our hats, so we can't possibly go to the party after all.'

'I beg your pardon, Teddy,' said Bruiny in a small voice. 'I'll make you some cocoa for tea.'

'And I beg your pardon, too,' said Teddy. 'I'll make you some toast for tea. We'll never quarrel again!'

But they did quarrel and do you know why? It was because Teddy couldn't find the toasting fork, so he toasted the bread on the end of the red umbrella! Bruiny was so angry, because he said the toast tasted of mud!

Well, well, well! You can't please some people, can you?

# The Toy Telephone

John had a toy telephone for his birthday. It was just like a real one, but the only thing wrong with it was that when John picked up the receiver and spoke into it, nobody answered him.

So he had to speak for himself and for the person he was speaking to as well. Sometimes he rang up the dog next door and sometimes he rang up his friends, and pretended to ask them to a party.

The telephone was green and had a place to speak into and a place to listen at. It stood on the table where John's farm was set out and looked very grand and grown-up.

One night a very strange thing happened. John was in bed, half asleep, when he heard the sound of little high voices in the nursery next to his bedroom. At first he thought he must be dreaming, then he knew he wasn't because he could hear the wind and the rain so clearly against the door.

'It surely can't be my *toys* that are talking together!' said John, feeling excited. 'No, it surely can't.'

He sat up in bed and listened. Yes, there was no doubt about it at all—there *were* people talking in the nursery and they had high bird-like voices, very sweet to listen to.

'I'm going to see who's there,' said John. He slipped on his dressing-gown and crept to the door. He went to the nursery and peeped in to see who was there, expecting to see his toys playing about.

But the toys were all exactly as he had left them! Most of them were in the toy cupboard, his teddy was in the armchair and the farm-yard was set out on the little table where the telephone stood.

John stared round the room. The fire was flickering and it wasn't difficult to see. And then John saw something rather surprising!

Sitting on the hearthrug, drying themselves, were four tiny creatures with wings. They were talking together in bird-like voices and John stared at them in the greatest surprise. At first he thought they were big moths, but soon he saw that they were pixies.

'Wow!' he said, going right into the room.

'I say! Who *are* you?'

The pixies sprang to their feet. But when they saw John's delighted face, they smiled up at him.

'We are four pixies, caught out in the rain,' said one, in a voice like a robin's, sweet and high. 'We flew in at the window to get dry. We *are* dry now—but we don't know whether to start out again or not, because if it goes on raining we shall get soaked. And Twinky here has already sneezed three times.'

Twinky sneezed a fourth time and the other pixies looked at him anxiously.

'I suppose you aren't any good at telling the weather, are you?' asked Twinky. John shook his head.

'No,' he said. 'I can never seem to tell if it is going to be fine or wet. If our grandpa were here, he could tell you, but he isn't. He always knows the weather.'

'Perhaps he knows the weather-clerk,' said Twinky. 'The weather-clerk lives up in the sky, you know, and always knows what weather is coming. I shouldn't be surprised if your grandpa is friends with him.'

'I don't think so,' said John, rather astonished. 'True, he always *does* look up at the sky when he

171

tells me what the weather is going to be—but he has never said anything to me about the weather clerk!'

'I wish we could telephone to the weather-clerk,' sighed Twinky. 'Then we should know what the weather will be for the rest of the night. We should know whether to stay here or whether to go on.'

John suddenly remembered his toy telephone. He reached it down from the table. 'Look!' he said. 'Here's a telephone! It's my own. You can use it if you like. But I must tell you that although it's easy to speak into it, it is very, very difficult to hear anyone talking back to you.

'Oh, we can easily get on to the weather-clerk by using a little magic!' cried Twinky, sneezing again. He rubbed the telephone all over with his tiny handkerchief and then spoke into it.

'Hello! Hello! Is that the weather-clerk? It is? Good! Then listen, Weather-clerk. This is Twinky the pixie speaking. It's just this minute stopped raining. Is it going to rain or blow any more tonight? If it isn't we can set out again in safety and go home.'

John heard a tiny voice talking back down the telephone, but he couldn't hear what it said.

*'Is that the weather-clerk?'*

Twinky heard though, and nodded round to the others. 'It's all right,' he said. 'We can go. There'll be no more rain tonight. Goodbye, John. And thank you so much for letting us use your telephone!'

Before John could say more than goodbye, the four tiny creatures flew out of the window and were gone in the dark night. John looked at his telephone. He picked up the receiver and spoke softly into it.

'Are you there still, Weather-clerk? Is it going to be fine tomorrow, because I want to have a picnic?'

A tiny voice answered him from far away. 'Yes, it will be fine tomorrow. You can have your picnic.'

'Oh, thank you!' said John joyfully, and crept back to bed. Sure enough the weather-clerk was right, and it *was* fine all the next day. And do you know, John *always* knows exactly what the weather is going to be, and I can guess why. It's because he can speak to the weather-clerk on his toy telephone whenever he wants to. Dear me, don't I wish he would lend it to me just for two minutes!

# Toy Town Adventures

Alison and Morris were going out for a picnic. They had their lunch in a basket and they meant to go to Windy Hill and eat it there. Windy Hill was a most exciting place. You could see a long way over the fields and lanes, and if you rolled a stone down, it would go bumping along right to the very bottom into the blue stream that curled round the foot of the hill.

'We'll roll some stones down before we eat our lunch,' said Morris. 'We'll see if we can make one splash into the stream at the bottom!'

So when they got to Windy Hill they found some big stones and sat down to roll them. One by one they bumped down Windy Hill, jumping high in the air as they went. It was great fun.

Alison found an extra big one and rolled it down—and dear me, when it got to some bushes a little way down the hill, they heard a loud yell and somebody rushed out of the bushes in fright. It was a little man and he disappeared round the hill, holding one of his arms with his hand.

'My stone hit him!' said Alison, in dismay. 'Oh dear, I didn't know there was anyone there! I do hope I haven't hurt him.'

'Didn't he look a funny little creature!' said Morris. 'Let's go and see if we can find him. We ought to say we're sorry.'

They went down the hillside to the bushes out of which the little man had run, but they couldn't see a sign of him anywhere around, until Morris spied a very strange thing!

It was a small wooden milk cart, with a wooden horse harnessed in front of it. In the cart were churns of milk.

'Oh, it's like a toy milk cart, just big enough to take children about,' said Morris. 'Do you think it belongs to that little man?'

'I don't know,' said Alison. 'Morris, let's get into the milk cart for a minute. It would be lovely to pretend it was ours.'

The two children got into the little milk cart and Morris took the lid off a churn to see if there was really milk inside. And just then, whatever do you think happened? The wooden horse looked round with a frightened face and called out: 'Oh, where's my master?'

The children were so astonished that they could say nothing at all and suddenly, the wooden horse began to gallop down the hill for all he was worth, the milk cart swinging behind him. The two children clung to the sides in fright and wondered whatever was going to happen.

Down the hill went the horse and at last came to an opening in the hillside. It was a cave, and into it he went at top speed.

'Wherever are we going?' shouted Morris to Alison. 'Try not to be frightened. I'll look after you!'

The cave narrowed into a passage which was lit by ball-shaped lamps all the way along. Now and again funny-looking little people flattened themselves against the wall to let the milk cart pass by, and looked after the children in surprise.

At last the passage came to an end and the horse galloped into what looked like a small square room. Here he stood still, panting, and the children were just going to get out, when suddenly the little room began to move upwards!

'Oh, it's a lift!' cried Alison in surprise. 'Goodness, whatever next? Wherever are we going to?'

Up and up the lift went and at last stopped. Before the children could get out, a large sliding door opened in front of the cart and out galloped the horse again at top speed, the children holding on to the sides tightly for fear of being shaken out.

And when they looked round they guessed where they were! It was Toy Town! All the houses were just like dolls' houses, and the shops were exactly like toy sweet shops. All kinds of toy animals walked about the streets, and in the distance was a toy fort with wooden soldiers parading round the battlements. It was really most exciting!

'What fun!' began Morris excitedly—but suddenly he stopped. A big stuffed policeman suddenly appeared from somewhere and held up his hand in front of the milk cart. The wooden horse stopped so quickly that the children fell in a heap on the floor of the cart.

'Now then, now then, what's all this?' said the policeman, taking out a large notebook. 'How dare you drive through Toy Town at this pace? You're breaking the law!'

'What fun!'

'We weren't driving. The horse was running away with us,' said Morris.

'I was running away because these children don't belong to my milk cart!' said the wooden horse, suddenly. 'They've stolen the cart and my master is lost, and I don't know where he is. Boo-hoo-hoo!'

'Oh, the story-teller!' cried Morris. 'We didn't steal the cart! We just got into it and the horse ran off.'

'What did you get into it for?' asked the policeman, writing in his notebook.

'Well—just to see how it felt to be in a toy milk cart,' said Alison.

'Seems a funny sort of reason,' said the policeman. 'I'm afraid you must give me your names and addresses and come with me. I must ask you some questions and see if we can find the real owner of the cart and hear what he has to say.'

'Never mind!' said Morris when Alison began to cry. 'It's all an adventure, Alison. Think what a fine tale we shall have to tell when we get home again!'

But Alison was really very frightened, especially when the stuffed policeman took out a big silver whistle and blew a loud blast on it. At once all the soldiers on the fort began to march out of the gateway and came in a straight line down the road towards the policeman.

'Are they coming to take us to the fort?' asked Morris.

'Yes,' said the policeman. 'But don't worry, the soldiers won't do you any harm. We haven't got a police station in Toy Town, so we always have to go to the fort with the soldiers.'

The toy soldiers surrounded the children and took them off to the fort. A crowd of dolls and toy animals stood on each side of the road and watched them go, chattering excitedly. Alison looked as brave as she could. She didn't want to cry in front of the toys!

The fort was just like Morris's toy fort at home. There was a sloping passage painted bright red, leading through a gateway. Inside the fort was a big room round which many more wooden soldiers stood, with their guns over their shoulders.

'I suppose they can't sit down because they are made of wood,' whispered Morris to Alison. 'There aren't any chairs at all!'

The captain sent one of the soldiers to fetch two chairs from the nearest dolls' house for the children to sit on. They sat down and then Morris remembered the picnic basket, which he had carried all the way with him!

'Hey, Alison! Let's have something to eat while we're waiting. I'm jolly hungry, aren't you?'

As soon as the toy soldiers saw the sandwiches, cakes, biscuits, chocolate and apples in the basket they crowded around.

'Ooh!' they cried, all together, and they looked so hungry that the children offered them some of their food.

'Thank you a thousand times!' cried the soldiers. 'We only get wood splinters to eat, you know, because we are made of wood, and this food is a real treat. The dolls have sawdust, of course—they are lucky—but, dear me, wouldn't they envy us if they saw us eating this simply scrumptious food!'

In a few minutes all the food was gone and the wooden soldiers thanked the children again and again for their treat. Just as Alison was brushing the crumbs off her frock, there came a noise outside the fort and the soldiers all sprang to attention.

'Soldiers! Bring the children to the Town Hall to be questioned!' cried the voice of the Captain as he entered the big room. All the soldiers saluted and the two children were marched out of the fort, down the street, and at last came to a wooden building with Town Hall written over the doorway.

Inside, behind a big table, sat a doll dressed as a judge. In front, sitting on twelve chairs in a wooden compartment, were twelve dolls and animals. They were the jury, who were to judge the children. In another place was a wooden milkman, his hand bound up in a bandage. The children knew that he was the little man who had been hit by their stone.

'Now,' said the judge, 'you two children are accused of three things—one, throwing a stone at this milkman; two—stealing his horse and cart; three—driving his horse and cart danger-ously through the streets of Toy Town. What have you to say for yourselves?'

'It is all a mistake,' said Morris, standing up very straight. 'We were on Windy Hill, rolling stones down to the stream at the bottom and one of them must have hit the poor milkman. It was quite an accident and we are very sorry. We ran down to tell him we were sorry, and saw his horse and cart. It was such a nice one that we thought we would like to get into it just for a moment.'

'The milkman says you stole it,' said the judge, looking at some notes in front of him.

'Well, we didn't,' said Alison, firmly. 'The horse took fright and ran away as fast as he could. He didn't stop until the policeman held up his hand in Toy Town. We were very frightened, I can tell you!'

'Where is the wooden horse? asked the judge. The horse was called for and, dragging his milk cart behind him, he came into the hall.

'Did you run away, or were you driven away?' asked the judge.

'I ran away!' stammered the horse.

'Did the children hurt you, or behave unkindly to you?' asked the judge.

'No!' said the horse. 'They didn't do anything except stand in the cart.'

'Ha!' said the judge, crossing something out in his notebook. 'It looks as if the children really didn't mean any harm—they were just meddlesome.'

'Please!' said the wooden milkman, popping up. 'I think they are unkind, cruel children. They hurt my hand with their stone!'

'Can anybody say whether or not these children are kind or unkind?' asked the judge, looking round the court . . . and all at once, every single one of the wooden soldiers who were in the court shouted at the tops of their voices:

'They're kind, they're kind! They shared their dinner with us and it was the most scrumptious food we have ever tasted!'

What a noise they made! The judge banged

on the table with his fist and at last the soldiers were quiet.

'Well, if the children really did share their dinner with the soldiers, it proves they are kind!' said the judge. 'What do you say, dolls and animals of the jury?'

'We say the same!' cried all the dolls and animals, jumping up and waving their hands and paws in the air.

The little milkman shouted too, and it seemed as if everyone in the hall was going quite mad!

'Let them go, they're kind! Let them go, they're kind!' cried everybody. Then the judge got out of his seat and went over to the children. He shook hands with them and told them they could go.

'The milkman will be pleased to drive you all the way home in his cart,' he said. 'He has quite forgiven you for everything.'

'Thank you,' said Alison, and Morris added: 'We'll come back again another day and bring all sorts of nice things for you to eat!'

Then everybody yelled again and Alison and Morris were taken out to where the milk cart stood beside the pavement outside. The judge shook hands with them again and off they went, the milkman driving in fine style.

It wasn't very long before they were at their front gate and they thanked the milkman very much.

'We hope your hand will soon be better,' said Morris, politely.

'Oh, the brownie who lives in the hillside near those bushes bound it up beautifully for me,' said the milkman with a smile. 'It will soon be all right. Goodbye.'

The children ran indoors to tell their mother where they had been and they begged her to come out and see the wooden milkman and his cart—but he had driven off, and all they could see was a cloud of dust in the distance.

'We're going to Toy Town again and we're going to take a great big basket of lovely things to eat!' said Morris, when they had finished telling Mummy all their adventures.

'You certainly shall,' said Mummy. 'I can't bear to think of those dolls and soldiers eating wooden splinters and sawdust, poor things! We'll go next week!'

I *do* wish I was going with them, don't you?

*The End*